I-35

BRETT SELMONT

Published in the United States of America

FIRST PAPERBACK EDITION

Library of Congress Cataloging-in-Publication Data

Selmont, Brett
I-35 / Brett Selmont
ISBN # 978-0-578-07011-7
I. Title.

Published by Detox Press
187 West End Ave.
New York, NY 10023

LUXURYROBOT

Designed by Luxury Robot

10 9 8 7 6 5 4 3 2 1

1

F looring the Lincoln south, I watched the speedometer climb like the late morning sun overhead. The vacant expressway provided little distraction beyond an occasional slab of roadkill and the odd patches of scrub brush that lined the asphalt. I eased on the accelerator, realizing that my haste to flee this bizarre state was not in my best interest. The last thing I needed was another altercation with the law.

Windows down, temperature in the sixties, a long way from the dreary skies and negative-nine degrees Minneapolis offered when I began this journey.

A large bug splattered on the windshield right in my sight line. Hitting the wipers, I was checking out the guts as they smeared across the glass in the shape of a rainbow when a sharp pain raced through my brain. I tried to maintain the road as my head turned migraine, sending the car into a swerve across the yellow line.

Up ahead on the left, I spotted what appeared to be an abandoned train car. My vision grew hazy, a phosphorus blur surrounded the structure, leaving the peripheral in focus. I blinked several times to adjust my sight but the illumination remained. Slamming on the brakes, I swerved into a parking lot, skidding across the dirt. A cloud of dust erupted into the air as the radiation around the train car zapped off like a television set and my headache subsided. The blurry vision returned to focus as I popped a Tramadol found on the passenger seat, chasing it with a sip of stale water.

Emblazoned across the side of the train car in bright red letters was, "The Railway Road Stop." I had been here before. Every detail seemed familiar, as if I'd built the diner myself. The white, spiral steel bars of the terrace at the back of the car, the wrought-iron ladder running up the front for accessing the roof, the long red flowerbed that ran the length of the car beneath the windows—I'd been here before.

I grabbed the gun from under the seat. Placing it in the back of my jeans, tucked neatly under my worn-in coffee-brown leather coat, I stepped out of the car and made my way toward the front door. A gust of wind swirled through the parking lot. Debris and pebbles pelted my face, stinging my skin like cheap aftershave. I shielded myself with my coat and entered.

Inside some truckers filled the counter space, putting the safety limits of the stools to the ultimate test. My eyes were drawn to a girl who sat alone in a corner booth against the windows. Above her head an electric exit sign blinked. The emergency door behind her was blocked by the booth—sacrificing safety for seating space.

Grabbing a stool between two truckers at the counter, using their girth as cover, I spied on the beauty in the corner. There was something reminiscent about the way her long, auburn hair swooped across the left side of her face, like a silky robin's wing. A lone emerald eye beamed out and she remained perfectly still, almost as if she were in a trance. Pillowy red lips perched from the surrounding milky skin. She was an exquisite painting hung on a dreary wall.

Her left arm was decorated with tattoos. A portrait of an expressionless young girl inside an ornate antique frame covered the curve of her shoulder and bicep in faded black and white. Bright red lips marked the child's face. On her forearm was another young, full-bodied girl whose head dwarfed her frame. This one was also black and white, except for the lips, which were cherry red. The tattoo girl brandished a whip as she bounced on a pogo stick.

The girl caught me watching her and flashed a glowing smile in my direction. A warm beam of recollection, it seemed. She wore three rusty gold necklaces, each one longer than the next. The shortest had three small triangle panels joined together to make one large one. It covered her bare chest. The next chain had a triangle that resembled the pyramid on the back of a dollar bill. The longest chain had three small elaborate triangles stretched roughly six inches apart.

She waved me over to her table. When I got closer I noticed the fingernails on her left hand were painted in a lush maroon, the same color of my car. As I slid across from her, my eyes focused on her antique gold watch. It was a man's watch; the stretchy gold band rode way up her left forearm. My father had one identical to it. Glancing down, I noticed the fingernails on her right hand were bare. She seemed to have two personalities at work, her left side mysterious, hidden by thick tresses, riddled with tattoos, her right exposed and naked for all to see.

"I like your dress," I said, making eye contact.

"Made it myself." She sat up, shimmying her torso to show off her handiwork.

The dress had frilly white lace straps that came over her bare shoulders and continued across the top of the bust line. Navy blue fabric with white polka dots draped comfortably below. It was feminine, girly, like she'd stolen it off a doll.

"So, what's a pretty girl like you doing in a place like this?" I charmed.

"You *really do* need ta work on your pickup lines," she said in a subtle southern drawl, brushing the hair from her face and revealing her left eye.

"What happened to your eyebrow?" I asked, a tinge of shock in my voice.

"That's funny," she said, wagging a packet of sugar in her fingers, settling the granules to the bottom of the pack.

"Why's that?"

"Are you serious?" she countered, ripping open the packet, pouring sugar into her coffee.

"Completely."

"You shaved it," she said frankly, clanking the spoon on the lip of the cup after she stirred.

"What?" I was astonished.

"You *don't* remember?"

"I have no idea what you're talking about," I responded, slightly amused by her gall.

"You said if I let you shave off my eyebrow," she pulled her hair back, revealing the bare skin above her eye again, "that you'd trust me. An' believe I'd really meet you here in one week."

Accenting her statement by holding up a finger, she continued, attempting to imitate a man's voice, "Cause you said people always say they'll be back but never follow through on it."

"And you let me?" I shot back, amazed.

"Obviously." She motioned to her missing eyebrow.

"What did I do for you?" I wondered, trying to gauge her level of sanity.

"You said you loved me," she stated, fearlessly.

"And that was enough?"

"I'm here, aren't I?" she snapped.

"And I said to meet me here? In this diner?" I chuckled, pointing to the table.

"Yeah, this date, this time, this diner, this fuckin' table in the corner."
She tapped both hands on the tabletop, spilling coffee on her saucer.

"Look, you're very attractive and probably a very sweet girl but I'm
afraid you're also very mistaken."

"Hey, Laurie-Anne?" she yelled to the waitress behind the counter.
"Can you bring over a decaf coffee?" She looked in my eyes and said,
"Black."

"Sure thing, sweetheart."

"That's how I take my coffee," I said.

"No shit, if you drink caffeine you'll bounce all over the restaurant
an'—" Simultaneously, we said, "Hang from the ceiling fan." I glanced
back at the fan in the center of the room.

"Exactly." She tilted her head to look around me, "Hey, Laurie-
Anne, you ev'r seen this boy b'fore?" she asked, releasing her drawl.

The waitress walked over with a cup of coffee on a saucer and placed
it on the table. She was a bulky woman with short, tight, curly black
hair, wearing a white T-shirt that read "Nobody Ever Raped A .38."
Black bullet-hole designs surrounded the slogan.

"Last week wit' y'all," she said. "I 'member cause you look like Kurt
Russell." She pointed at me with her pen. "Member, I say's to ya, you
look just like that movie star Kurt Russell?"

"An' then he ordered a black decaf coffee," the girl proposed.

"That's right!" The waitress squealed, "Also, you two was neckin'
pretty serious." She began walking away. "Don't forget that too easy,"
she called back to us. Some of the truckers turned and smiled. They
looked at the waitress with peculiar facial expressions. The waitress
shrugged her shoulders.

"Look, this is some kind of a joke, right? You and her." I pointed to
the waitress. "You do this to people, fuck with them?"

"Honey, how did I know the way you take your coffee?"

"Lucky guess?" I wondered aloud.

She took a frustrated breath, sipped her coffee, then continued her interrogation. "Is your name David?"

"Yeah." I nodded.

"An' in your car," she brought her voice to a whisper, leaning in across the table and looking me in the eyes. "Do you have a shitload a' cocaine?"

"How do you know that? Are you a cop? Have you been following *me*?!" I growled.

"No!" she shouted back. Some of the truckers turned, raised their eyes.

"Look," she returned to a whisper. "On the tip a' your penis, you got a lil ol' beauty mark?"

"How do you know this?" I demanded.

"Cause we had sex on like twenty separate occasions!" she screeched. The truckers turned again, laughing. One of them made a funny face and circled his temple with his index finger, to say we were crazy. His buddy cracked up.

The girl squeezed my hand tightly across the table and reasoned, "How'd a cop know that?"

I stared at her hand, focusing on the chipped nail polish just beyond the tips of her fingers. She gave my hand another reassuring squeeze on the table.

The only thing I could truly trust in this world was that I was sitting in a diner right now on the edge of Oklahoma. And four days ago, I woke up in Minnesota and traveled to this point.

PART
ONE
LIMBO

2

The sun peeked above the landscape spreading daylight through the tinted windows of my grandfather's Lincoln Continental. I awoke, shaking and bleary-eyed, and felt the cold air encircle me. My right calf ached as I stretched it along the plush maroon leather of the backseat.

Where was I?

Outside a fortress of snow embankments encased the small gravel parking lot behind a rundown apartment complex. I rubbed my stiff neck, attributing the soreness to the confined sleeping quarters or, perhaps, the hunched driving position I had assumed all night. For the life of me, I could not remember how I'd gotten here.

Crawling between the seats to the front of the car, I turned the ignition, fired up the engine and cranked the heat to max. Cold exhaust rushed from the vents, propelling a stale, scented air reminiscent of crayon around the car. Looking in the rearview mirror, I pushed aside my tangled brown hair and rubbed the morning crust from the corner of my eyes. The ashtray overflowed with cigarette butts and the fuzzy floor mat on the passenger side was littered with pills, empty water bottles, beer cans, paper coffee cups and junk food wrappers, a filthy homage to life on the road. I must have been traveling for days.

Fiddling with the radio dial, I prayed it would work. The finicky antenna extended outside the Lincoln as a deep voice bellowed through the rectangular chrome speakers on the dashboard.

It's seven o'clock in the morning and bitterly cold ALL across the metro today. High temperatures expected to be ONLY in the low single digits again. Right now it's minus nine with the windchill here on the second day of March, which truly is adhering to the old axiom of entering like a lion...Let's hope that the lamb isn't too far behind. Another man's voice chimed in, *I'm afraid the lion ate the lamb, Jack.*

Ha, ha, Phil, don't say that. I have a feeling global warming isn't coming to the Twin Cities anytime soon.

Second day of March. What happened to the last 72 hours?

My blackout wasn't all that alarming. I was prone to serious headaches that sometimes led to a loss of consciousness. Over the years I've ended up in some peculiar places, but it was more like sleepwalking. How I wound up halfway across the country was bewildering, to say the least.

Huddled in the driver's seat, shivering, waiting for the heat to kick in, the dizzy specter of a migraine lingering between my ears. I reached over to the passenger's seat, swiping aside the debris, and found an empty, translucent orange bottle of Tramadol that rested beneath a Snickers wrapper.

With my frozen fingers, I picked two football-shaped tablets from the passenger seat, tossed the pills past my blue-tinged lips and swallowed without the aid of water. Tramadol was a painkiller prescribed to cancer patients but doctors found that it also had positive effects on migraine headaches and certain types of anxiety disorders. I suffered from both at the moment. Tramadol also helped to alleviate my skeleton's aversion to the restrictive and suffocating nature of my skin. When I felt the restless bone-rattling commence and the sharp tug of my lips wanting to peel back over my skull, I knew it was time to take a pill.

On the passenger's seat, an open notebook listed my brother's address in Minneapolis. I carried a notebook at all times to categorize certain thoughts, feelings and, occasionally, to check my whereabouts in the event of a blackout. This was something I'd done for years, a habit suggested to me by a psychologist as a way to keep my turbulent life from falling into complete disorder. I must have been in a hurry, judging by the scrawling way I'd written the address.

Gingerly thumbing through the pages of my journal, waiting for the feeling in my fingertips to return, I noticed the last entry was dated February 27th. This was followed by three blank pages, then my brother's scribbled address, with the date March 2nd written in the header.

As the vents circulated warm air through the cab, my blood flow returned, throbbing to the tips of my fingers. Grabbing my cell-phone from the passenger seat, I flipped open the screen and searched my most recent calls. All of them were made to my brother Jim.

I dialed my voicemail, punched in the secret code and waited. There was one saved message from my brother on February 28th at 1:04 A.M.

The only decipherable words amongst the static and terrifying screams were my name, *David*, and the words *children, devil, tattoos, one,* and *I-35,* followed by a woman's gut-wrenching scream in the background.

"PLEASE GOD NO!" Jim's voice sounded as if it was coming through a distortion pedal. It barely resembled him, but I knew it was him.

I replayed the voicemail and scribbled the words I could understand into my notebook. When I heard the bloodcurdling screams again, I knew this wasn't some kind of prank. The rapid beat of my heart pumped blood through my body and the cold I felt before was replaced with a rush of fear and adrenaline.

Until six months ago, my older brother and I hadn't spoken to each other in over ten years. Jim contacted me out of the blue, saying that he wanted to apologize for abandoning me years ago. It was an awkward exchange and gave me the impression that I was number nine in a 12-Step program. Our conversation was brief; he did most of the talking and informed me about his life. He'd been living in Minneapolis, married his wife Charlotte five years ago, and they were in a traveling bluegrass band called The Carnies. He explained that his travels rarely took him to New York City—there wasn't much demand for a two-piece country-bluegrass band in Manhattan—and that his tours usually consisted of driving up and down the I–35 highway from Minneapolis to Austin. We made a little small talk, Jim told me a few stories about gigs he'd played, and ended the conversation by saying that if he was ever in New York we should grab a beer. Then he informed me he had to go pack up his van for some Bluegrass festival in West Virginia.

I couldn't imagine that we would ever see each other again. Our lives had gone in different directions, and sentimentality was never one of our strong points. But apparently I'd packed a knapsack, hopped in my late grandfather's old maroon Lincoln Continental and driven west to Minneapolis even though I didn't remember doing it. And I doubt I would have come at all if it hadn't been for the chilling message I received in the wee hours of the morning on February 28th.

3

F rantically calling my brother's cell phone several times to no response, I fled the warm confines of the Lincoln's womb and rang the buzzer for his apartment. A yellow police warning was taped to the front door, notifying the residents of 204 Franklin Avenue of recent robberies in the area. The lock on the front door was broken and I walked right in. I guess the landlord thought a police warning was enough to deter crime. Hideous furry orange carpeting, a relic of '70s interior design, lined the stairway to Jim's apartment on the second floor. The walls swirled with coarse stucco, the kind that scraped your arms and left a sandy white residue. A drip from the ceiling made the carpet in front of Jim's apartment smell like an old Saint Bernard.

I knocked hard on the thick walnut door, waited briefly for a response, then rapidly pounded again. When no one came, I made my way back outside.

The environment in Minnesota was drastically different from the East Coast. Cold here was severe, arctic. I could feel my nose hairs crystallize as I inhaled. My breath clouded the air like cigarette smoke and a chill seeped deep into my bones. Luckily, there was only a slight wind. The winter sea breezes off the coast of Rhode Island, where I was raised, could be nasty. The wicked winds that funneled through the streets of Manhattan made New York City winters harsh. But this was something I'd never experienced. It was a bitter cold, an enemy that swooped down from Canada, shocking your system, viciously freezing everything in its path. This was Jack London shit, bleak and desolate, with the warm dream of a remedy too far in the distance to be therapeutic.

After calling my brother's cell again and leaving an anxious message, I returned to the Lincoln to find a note placed under the windshield wiper.

These parking spaces are for 204 Franklin St. residents only! Please do not park here or your car will be towed immediately!

Walking over to another car, placing the note under the windshield, I was impressed by my demeanor. Normally, I'd have let my anger boil through my bloodstream and up to my brain. My brain would then notify my body to erupt in a physical display, one that usually ended with smashed windows or broken bones, especially when I was in a position of vulnerability like I was now. But calmly, I returned to the Lincoln, blasted the heat and ran my hands in front of the vents again as the warm air returned the blood to my fingers.

The sun went silent behind a field of clouds, casting a jaundiced tint over the Minneapolis morning. Jim's life was a mystery to me, as was the city I drove through at the moment. Eastward on Franklin Avenue, no particular destination, the periphery of Minneapolis seemed to consist mostly of two- and three-story houses and brick apartment complexes. I passed a welfare building a few blocks from my brother's place. A long line of unfortunates stretched out of the building into the cold. Their day got even worse as a Channel 5 news van pulled up for the morning feature.

My brother obviously lived in the classy section of town. Next to the welfare building was a boarded-up Dairy Queen. A tall sign on a post out front read, "WE GOT CAKES." My pessimistic mind mixed with the slummy neighborhood and I immediately believed it was a cryptic message from a drug dealer to his clientele, alerting them that the new shipment of crack had arrived.

A rusted old car with no tires rested on blocks in the parking lot of a 24-hour convenience store named Super America.

I made a right on Nicollet Avenue, heading south toward downtown Minneapolis. Ahead were glass skyscrapers connected by skyways. This, I believed, was to keep the faithful warm during the brutal winters so they didn't have to venture outside to move from building to building. During our conversation, my brother mentioned getting lost once on his way to a gig in the underground tunnels at the University of Minnesota. He said it got so cold the students used the tunnels to travel to class during winter. Perhaps that's why their mascot was a gopher.

I pulled into an open parking space without knowing why and exited the Lincoln. Outside, the sidewalk was a sheet of ice. Buttoning my long, leather coat, wishing I'd brought a pair of gloves, I reached into my pocket for a lighter and lit a smoke. The cold air attacked my skin like a school of piranha. A tight burn began to run through my fingers and I nearly wiped out on the rigid ice beneath me. I passed a Middle Eastern restaurant called Jerusalem, a dingy African eatery, and a little Vietnamese joint with a handwritten sign in black magic marker that read, PHO QUAN. The sign boasted, BEST SOUP TOWN.

All along Nicollet, signs stated, WELCOME TO EAT STREET. Minneapolis had more variety, both in cuisine and ethnicity, than I expected; Chinese and Korean markets colored the treacherous sidewalk. After passing a large Army Navy store, I slid on the skating rink they called a street to the front door of The Ganges Coffee shop.

I warmed myself with a cup of black decaf I held in both hands to calm my shakes. The pink-haired pixie barista had a large, black star tattoo on her neck and silver metal studs in her cheeks. The studs sunk into her dimples as she spoke in a thick Minnesota accent.

"Sure is cold out there, ya know."

I nodded agreement and made my way to a table near the windows, sitting down to face the front door. Turning my head to the street, I had a terrific view of all the buses and polluted snow that covered Nicollet Avenue. My sympathy went out to the ill-fated Minnesotans who needed public transportation. They stood somberly, shivering at a bus stop enveloped by a veil of frozen exhale.

A punk rocker with a shaved head, wearing lots of leather and spikes, sat a few tables away. He glanced up from his copy of *Profane Existence: Making Punk a Threat Again,* and we locked eyes for a moment before he returned to his magazine. At another table cluttered with books sat a bespectacled fellow draped in a heavy green and white flannel shirt and thick brown corduroys. His bulky black snow boots rested in a puddle on the floor. He had a neatly trimmed beard, which he scratched lightly with his fingertips while concentrating on a very thick book. I took a sip of my coffee, and glanced around the coffee shop. In the corner of the room with their backs to me were a man in a cowboy hat and an incredibly heavy woman sitting in a wheelchair.

A stack of free newspapers sat in a kiosk by the front door. Piles of flyers for rock shows and upcoming events covered a table next to the newspapers. Several drab pastel paintings hung on the north white wall. In one of the paintings, half a rotted watermelon was sliced open, the demon-eyed pits appearing to rise above the canvas in an optical illusion. In another, there was a dreary peach with a quarter sliced out, the nook-and-cranny pit leaping from the center of the painting that was reminiscent of Warhol's celebrity art. Only dead fruit played the role of the pop culture icon. On a black-and-white Elliot Smith poster, one of the corners peeled from the wall, someone wrote "IS HERE" in black marker below his name. Another poster, this one for an animal rights rally being held in a place called The Rock Garden, hung beside it. Below the posters rested an unoccupied, fraying green couch and a burgundy coffee table. They looked like they'd been bought from a yard sale or borrowed from someone's parents' basement. A small black stage filled the back alcove next to a door that read: *Staff Only.* The thought of monotonous poetry readings, political outrage and bad singer-songwriters strumming acoustic guitars made my skin feel itchy. This *is* the city where Bob Dylan began after all. The high ceiling, modern lighting and stark white walls of the space seemed more appropriate for an internet café than the homey coffee shop they attempted to create. Sparse decoration and an eclectic feel gave the impression of a business in transition or recently opened. I made my way over to the table near the front door and grabbed a *City Pages*. After searching the music section for my brother's band and finding nothing, I ripped out a page that contained all of the names of venues and addresses in town. I stuffed it in my pocket as I exited the coffee shop.

4

MONDAY, MARCH 2ND
MINNEAPOLIS, MINNESOTA

———————

Triple Rock, City Billiards, The Viking, 400 Club, First Avenue, 7th Street Entry, The Turf Club, Terminal Bar, Lee's Liquor Bar, The Cabooze, Moose and Sadie's, Williams, Uptown Bar, Club Underground, The Fine Line, C.C. Club—I stopped at every club or bar I found in *The City Pages*.

Most locals I encountered on my tour of the Twin Cities were grounded in melancholy. Worried about surviving their harsh environment but knowing the cruel winter would be endured and replaced with happier times. Their satisfaction was brief, however, at the realization that this march of the penguins was a perennial event.

The natives contributed little to my search. Behind stoic façades, those who would admit they knew anything about Jim and Charlotte scratched their flaky scalps, glanced at their shoes, and corroborated each other's stories as if they had rehearsed for a trial. The general consensus was that my brother and his wife were decent people and talented musicians who kept to themselves.

Night had fallen on the Twin Cities. The Midwestern sky was a blanket of darkness and the temperature on a digital clock outside the North Fork Bank rounded to zero degrees. I was no closer to finding my brother than when I'd listened to his hellish message in the early morning. My paranoid disposition and years of absorbing horror films forced brutal images to mind: my brother, his wife, the sharp edge of an axe slicing through the moonlight, wads of human flesh splattering against an old barn door.

My hands began to tremble, partly from anxiety, partly from the cold as I squeezed the steering wheel and turned off Lyndale Avenue on to Franklin. It was just past 9:00 P.M. and I felt like the Omega Man. The street was deserted as I passed the 24-hour Super America with the rusted-out car in the parking lot, passed the boarded-up Dairy Queen and the coded crack out front, then sped by the empty welfare building, parking the Lincoln in a closed-down gas station across the street from Jim's apartment.

Popping the trunk, I grabbed a tire iron and hid it beneath my coat. Snow flurries rifled through the green, yellow and red rainbow of the stoplight as I crossed Franklin Avenue to the icy sidewalk in front of Jim's building.

Scraggly bushes lined the walkway, thick, unflattering shrubs that seemed to dominate the landscape of Minneapolis' less fortunate neighborhoods. They were cheap and sturdy, probably the only vegetation that could survive the cruel winters. I ignored the warning taped to the window and entered the building. Making my way up the furry orange carpeting to the second floor, I slid the bezel end of the tire iron into the gap between Jim's door-jamb just below the deadbolt lock. Using the tire iron like a crowbar, I adjusted my grip, throwing all of my weight forward onto the shaft. A loud crack filled the hallway as the door popped open.

Their apartment was a castle. The large living room stretched into a huge adjoining dining room with lush hardwood floors. A teal antique couch with curved, dark wooden legs rested against the wall. Incense sticks burned in decorative wooden trays on a redwood coffee table. A rainbow-colored bong sat on a small table with a pile of unwrapped tree-shaped air fresheners and more incense. The table looked like a tree stump with a door and resembled something you'd find in the home of a Hobbit. The far wall of the dining room was crammed with musical equipment: microphones, amps, guitars, a banjo, ukulele and a tambourine. Down a short hallway to the right was a decent kitchen with faux bark cabinets and a red linoleum floor. The open shelves were filled with couscous, wheat germ, tempeh, and a bunch of Amy's Organic soups, and clear plastic bags of basmati rice, brown rice and bulgur wheat. To the left of the kitchen was their bedroom. I didn't come across any clues, only more candles, incense and endless piles of clothing, women's shoes and underwear on the floor. The mess surrounded the mattress they used as a bed. It was like they'd just come into the room, stripped and fallen into bed.

Walking back through the living room, I saw a room at the front of the apartment. It was a small office. Wood paneling surrounded two wind-rattled windows overlooking the street. A small electric heater was set into the wall under non-weatherproofed windows. I searched through the huge filing cabinet they called an office which was covered with old newspapers, sheet music and lyrics. Sifting through the clutter, nervously trying to speed up my effort, I found a print-out for the South by Southwest Music Festival in Austin, Texas. It was dated March 12th thru the 19th. I found nothing else of consequence.

Another door off the living room was locked. I figured it was where they kept their more expensive music equipment. Placing the tire iron in the door-jamb I pried the door open easily, shattering the cheap wood molding that lined the entrance. A long black ergonomic table and matching chairs that didn't fit with the earthy, hippy style of the rest of the apartment were centered in the sparse room. On the table were two small scales, one manual and one electric. To the left of the scales were hundreds of tiny glassine baggies and a two-by-two black metal box secured with a small gold lock. Slamming the crowbar down on the lock I sent the box flying from the table, crashing to the floor. A large plastic bag filled with loose white powder fell to the ground. I picked up what felt like a pound of cocaine, grabbed the tire iron and hurried out of the room.

A sturdy man several inches taller than me stood barefoot in the dining room, wearing blue jeans and a white T-shirt. He held a gun and pointed it in my direction.

"Put down the weapon and get your hands up. Put 'em where I can see 'em," the man stated loudly, but calmly.

I dropped the bag of coke and the tire iron, which clanked to the ground. The man had a buzz cut, his face blocked by his hands and the gun so I couldn't get a good look at him. He had round, powerful shoulders and his triceps protruded from beneath his tight white T-shirt.

"Get against the wall, asshole!" he ordered.

I obeyed, turning and placing my hands on the wall near the door to the room as I searched my mind for a plan.

"Spread 'em!" He inched closer, still pointing the gun at me.

I spread my legs. He came up behind me, shoving me into the wall. With his free hand he checked my legs, pointing the gun up toward my head with his other hand.

"Wait, I can explain!" I shouted back.

"Keep your fucking eyes on the wall!" he demanded, continuing to frisk me, working his way up to my waist.

"I live here! I lost my keys!" I pleaded.

"Bullshit," he yelled. "I live downstairs. I know everybody in this complex. You don't live here."

"Look, I'm just visiting…"

"Shut your mouth!"

"Let me explain," I begged.

"Shut up now or I will shoot you," he threatened, smashing my face into the wall. "Is that your maroon car across the street?" he asked, moving his free hand up my side.

"Yeah, look, I told you I'm just visiting!" His hand checked under my armpit. I pushed forward, creating a little separation from the wall. I could feel his shitty cop breath on the back of my neck.

"I almost had that piece of shit towed away this morning," he informed. "I had a feeling whoever owned that car was casing the joint."

"Please, sir, my brother..."

He cut me off.

"You're going downtown."

I heard the clang of metal as he pulled handcuffs from his pocket.

"You don't look like the normal scumbags around here." He relaxed a bit as he pulled my left arm back to attach the handcuff. I could tell he underestimated me because of our difference in size. The cold metal of the cuff hit my wrist and he got ready to clasp it. I bent my neck forward, touching my chin to my chest.

"Most of the fucks we get around here are niggers and drunk Indians."

I swung my head back full force and exploded the back of my skull into his nose. I could feel the cartilage crush against the middle of my head. The gun and cuffs flew from his hands to the floor of the dining room. Turning, I watched as his legs slowly buckled and he dropped to the floor. Instinctively, he grabbed his nose with both hands as the blood seeped through the cracks of his fingers. Before he could regain his composure I came down hard with a right hand to his face, sending a splattering of blood to the ground, slamming the back of his skull into the hardwood floor, knocking him unconscious. I cuffed his right hand and dragged his limp body into the living room, leaving a bloody trail. I wrapped the chain around the radiator pole and attached the other cuff to his left hand.

In the kitchen, I rifled through the cabinets till I found a blue recycling bag. I ran to the second bedroom, tossed the coke into the bag, then picked up the gun and the tire iron from the corner of the dining room. On my way out the door, I snatched a small framed picture of Jim and Charlotte standing in front of a place called The Corn Palace. Then I stopped, walked over to the bloody cop and kicked him in the ribs. He curled into a fetal position and with my free hand I took his wallet from the back pocket of his jeans. A police badge might come in handy. Glancing back, I watched as blood slowly painted his face. The smell of burning hair scented the room as the hot radiator pole singed his arm. I turned off the lights, shut the door as best I could and ran out through the frozen night to the Lincoln.

Driving south a hundred miles an hour on I-35, I wondered how Jim, a pot-smoking naturalist who played down-home music, could push such a hard drug. Did those drugs have something to do with the terrifying voicemail I received?

5

A lone on the highway, driving through the darkness of Iowa, I had one eye on the road ahead and one on the rearview mirror. My best guess was that Jim and Charlotte were on tour. The only clue that made sense to me on the voicemail was "I-35." During our conversation Jim mentioned they traveled that highway frequently on their way to gigs all over the Midwest. This wasn't much of a lead. I had roughly 1,200 miles of road to cover that stretched the middle of America from North to South. My anxiety intensified with each click of the odometer. Lack of sleep began to feed my paranoia.

What the fuck happened to Jim?

What the fuck happened to me for three days?

Were the police on my ass yet?

There was almost nothing I despised more in this world than cops. As I sped along the Iowa asphalt, watching the dotted line of the highway blur into one continuous stripe, I recalled when my distrust of law enforcement turned to hatred.

It was the perfect summer evening. A reddish purple haze floated above the bright tangerine bulb of sun. A group of seagulls cawed in the sky and the smell of ocean scented the air. I had just hit a double and stood on second base proudly. Beyond the chain fence that surrounded the baseball diamond, on the beach across the street, I could see all the other boys playing with pretty girls. None of them paid any attention to the game. They were having too much fun to care that I'd just crushed a ball to the gap in right centerfield.

Baseball, to me, was an old man's game. I wanted to spend my summers riding bikes and chasing girls, not pop flies. At that moment I turned to the other team's shortstop and declared, "This sucks. I'm quitting after the game, man."

He laughed, and replied, "Me too."

After the game we hopped in the family car. My dad was driving slowly, as usual, one hand on the steering wheel, the other cupping the tan half-bowl of his trusty pipe. My mom sat next to him, holding a long, slender white Bel Air 100 out the window. My brother sat in back next to me, playing a portable game of Asteroids. Getting pizza after little league games was a family tradition, and the only thing I figured I'd miss about baseball.

At the restaurant, I tore into a slice of pepperoni pizza. But I couldn't enjoy the moment because I was fixating on how to tell my father that I wanted to quit baseball.

My father wasn't a pushy sports dad; his main goal was for Jim and me to be happy. But I was still troubled that he'd perceive me as a quitter. I knew he'd try to talk me out of it. My father, with his kind, deep voice, had a way with words and people. He could have been mayor if he chose, but he was too honest to be a politician. He had a calm, trusting air about him and people felt comfortable around him. This was why he was the vice president of the Elk's Club, an influential men's association in town. His easy speaking manner made him a terrific history teacher and, now, the respected head of guidance counseling at Providence University. His eloquent speech and reassuring tone were also how he convinced my mom to marry him. My dad was a short stout man, with a long nose and bushy brown sideburns. His looks and middle class means wouldn't have been enough to persuade my mother. But he had a charming sense of humor, gleeful laugh, and his advice was so charitable and earnest it could have spewed from an old black-and-white sitcom.

My mother was a beautiful woman, tall and slender with chestnut hair. She needed no makeup to bring out the glitter in her almond-shaped eyes. At parties I'd hear grown-ups compare her to Audrey Hepburn, though my mom would always remind me of Jaclyn Smith from "Charlie's Angels," minus the judo prowess and firearms training. My mother had a sophisticated style but she wasn't ostentatious: sleek turtleneck sweaters paired with comfortable, earth-toned slacks, a pair of small diamond stud earrings. She exuded the classy conservative aura of the young mother who was still fashionable as she squired two unruly boys around town.

The other quality I loved about her was her uncanny ability to remain calm when chaos surrounded her. Her temperament was second to none. Maybe it was the fact that Jim and I, especially the latter, were such a handful. Or it could have come from her being raised in the hectic hustle and bustle of New York City. I never saw her become angry, or flustered, no matter the circumstance.

When my father and mother met in New York she had marriage proposals from millionaires and big-time executives. She worked for Universal Studios before they relocated to Hollywood. She had visions of being Diane Sawyer or Barbara Walters. But my father, in his smooth, self-assuring way, convinced her they'd have a better life on the beach in Rhode Island far away from everyone and everything she knew, away from the chaotic and exciting life of the city. And my father was right. They were happy; we were happy. My parents had an enviable marriage. It had nothing to do with money, or expensive toys, or any type of privilege. It had to do with respect. They treated our friends, no matter how young, like real people.

I ate my pizza joylessly, then put down my crust and told my parents that I was quitting baseball. Nobody said anything for a while. They continued to eat, my mom using a knife and fork to cut her slice of plain pizza into bite-sized pieces. Off in his own world, Jim shoveled down a greasy slice of pepperoni. My dad sipped his drink, then checked the time on his gold stretch-band watch.

After a moment, my dad broke the silence.

"If that's what you want to do," he paused.

I focused on the faded brown coffee stains on his bottom teeth as he spoke softly.

"I'm not going to tell you otherwise, but I think you should consider this from every angle before you decide. You made a commitment to your team. This is a big decision and it affects more than just you. You realize that, right?"

I nodded, but of course I'd thought about nobody else. The only thing I was interested in was getting out of baseball practice.

The rest of the dinner was quiet and everyone remained silent as we piled into the car to head home. My mom lit a cigarette. She used to write a note for the store clerk and I'd ride my bike down to Hubbard's to buy her cigarettes. She would always let me keep the change so I could buy candy or play whatever video game they featured that summer. My father took some tobacco out of his pouch of Captain Black and packed his pipe, lighting it with a beat-up Zippo. I loved the chocolatey aroma of the burning tobacco that filled the car. Jim sat next to me as we backed out of the parking spot. The only sounds in the car were the beeps and explosions from Jim's game.

In the backseat of the car, I decided that continuing to play baseball was way better than how I felt right now. I would stay on the team. As we pulled onto the street, I called, "Dad!"

He glanced back, the black stem of the pipe between his teeth. Smoke puffed from the corner of his mouth.

"I think I'm gonna keep playing baseball."

"Mmmhmm," he mumbled, dangling the pipe from his lips, never seeing the speeding police cruiser as it annihilated the driver's side of the car.

Everything happened so fast. It was as if I was watching it on TV. My mother and father were silent; the silly beeping of the game still played between bursts of Jim's screams. My head was wobbly but I was pretty much unharmed. I called out for my father several times at the top of my lungs, trying to get a response from the twisted metal before me. He never responded. My father died on impact.

I watched from the curb as Jim was placed on a stretcher and loaded into an ambulance with a broken leg. My mom, unconscious, still lay in the wreckage, while orange and blue sparks flew from the car like Fourth of July fireworks. Firemen in heavy black coats sawed through the steel frame and door of the car with the jaws-of-life.

My mother was carefully taken out of the ruins by paramedics and placed on a board, decorated in my father's blood. They used velcro straps to secure her body, applied a foam neck brace, lifted her onto the stretcher and loaded her into an ambulance. My vision was blurred; everything I saw was fluctuating between reality and fluorescent yellow. A paramedic with long, curly brown hair came over to me. I remember questions being asked, but I just stared at my father's lifeless, mangled body, glancing over occasionally at the two policemen who killed him. They sat on the back of an ambulance, their identities hidden behind oxygen masks. Their uniform shirts were unbuttoned, the white T-shirts beneath still looking dryer-fresh. The paramedic touched my forehead and spun me around gently. "You're bleeding," she exclaimed. I touched the side of my head, brought my hand down and looked at the dark, fluorescent yellow-substance covering my hand. The ambulance with my mom inside pulled away and I stood on the curb, bleeding from my skull, still wearing my stupid orange baseball uniform.

6

A white stream of jet exhaust blazed a line through the night and clung to the bottom of the crescent-shaped moon. My eyes shifted from the heavens and returned to earth, focusing on the highway ahead. My quick stop in Des Moines revealed a ghost town. The streets were vacant and eerily silent for a metropolitan hub at night. The few people I encountered shuffled through town like the living dead. Most were dressed in drab clothing and puffy parkas. The few who looked up from the ground and engaged with me spoke in monotone half-sentences. It was as if the entire city was on Nyquil. I filled my tank with economy regular, $4.06 a gallon, and decided it was best to flee this place as quickly as possible for fear of the authorities. Besides, nothing was happening anyway. Tuesday night in Des Moines was really Sunday morning in disguise.

Driving towards Kansas City I wondered if anyone had received an APB about me yet. Alone, in the dark, and confused, I let my thoughts drift back to the torture that was adolescence.

My mother survived the accident but was paralyzed from the waist down. She had the use of her left arm, nearly none in her right. My brother recovered from his broken leg and began his junior year of high school. I was entering ninth grade with the burden of taking care of my paraplegic mother, a daunting task. My mom was an only child, and her parents passed away so long ago I could barely remember them. My father had a few relatives scattered about the country, but none geographically or emotionally close enough to provide assistance. We were forced to grow up fast, or in this case, to do grown-up things fast. Neither Jim nor I were emotionally ready for such a tragedy. There was no training, guide book or class that could prepare us for this at any age, let alone at 14 and 16.

We did what was necessary for our mother's survival. We made meals, fed her, got her tea, combed her hair, lit her cigarettes. The doctors ordered her to stop smoking but I bought them for her anyway. She didn't have anything to live for and I wasn't going to take away her lone pleasure in life. Jim and I did laundry, cleaned, dusted, washed dishes, organized her medications, brought her water to wash them down. We carried out every conceivable act but bathing and dressing her; a registered nurse came by a few hours a day, after we left for school. Most of my nights were spent watching TV with my mom and wiping the drool from her mouth before we put her to bed.

My mother's condition worsened. Eventually her hair fell out due to complications from her medication. It was weird when she went bald. The accident had claimed the last of her womanhood. She didn't even resemble a woman anymore, nor did she feel like one. Just a bald, one-armed, semi-human being confined to a wheelchair. She felt like she was a burden to me, and the world.

Nothing happened to the cops who killed my dad and paralyzed my mother. They were absolved of all charges, everything from manslaughter to reckless driving. They didn't even get suspended. I heard rumors around town that they'd been drinking, and that they hit us at twice the legal speed limit. We didn't get any money from the cops, the town, not even from the Elk's Club. My father didn't have life insurance so we had to sell our house and move into a small apartment on the other side of town to pay for the medical bills that exceeded our coverage. Everything had changed. Both my parents were essentially dead, and Jim was becoming a stranger to me. We stopped communicating. It was like he'd lost the ability to speak to me in the accident. Jim was always more sensitive than I was and had a very close relationship with our mom. Although he was two and a half years older than me, Jim was quite small in stature. With his frail body and long hair, elderly people often mistook him for a girl. Jim couldn't play any sports well or defend himself in a fight. Because of this he was a bit of an outcast in school.

Our situation began to take its toll on Jim emotionally. He'd cry in his bedroom alone almost daily. At a time when he needed support, to know that someone in the world cared for him, I did the opposite. My frustration with the world made me angry and Jim was an easy target. I mistook his sensitive nature and small stature as weakness and ridiculed him for it. Eventually, he completely checked out. Unable to see our mother in such a disabled state and incapable of dealing with my mood swings, he packed his bags and disappeared before his senior year of high school.

After Jim ran away I began rebelling against teachers and had to resist the temptation to go on a town-wide killing spree. I wanted to bomb the place. It took every ounce of willpower not to seek revenge on those cops. I told my mom once that I was going to kill them. She didn't respond.

My migraines and occasional blackouts began to increase. I spent my nights staying up with insomnia or twisting and turning from my nightmares. Most of my dreams involved my being someone like Jack the Ripper and cutting those cops into pieces, or wearing a hockey mask and stalking members of my father's club with a chainsaw. I'd wake up grinding my teeth or on the floor or in other rooms of the house, even the backyard once. Half-asleep and not knowing where I was, I'd attempt to scream but wouldn't be able to. It was like I lived constantly inside a sound-proof cocoon.

During this period, I'd lost all interest in school work. My honor roll grades had been replaced with threats of being left back. I started to drink alcohol daily, smoked my mom's cigarettes and stole her pain medication. I drank anything I could get my hands on. I'd even worked out a way to buy my own liquor. The owner of a package store, Jack, knew about my situation. His store was right next to the pizza place where the accident happened. I told him I was buying alcohol for my mom because she couldn't get it herself. Not that doctors would have let her drink in her condition. Jack knew this but was sympathetic because of my situation.

My mom had lost the will to live, and her body finally agreed. She died of heart failure when I was 16, just as I was set to begin my junior year of high school. This was the third high school I'd attended in three years. The first school change was because we moved to a new district, the second because I was expelled for fighting. Having lost all respect for authority and education, the only goal I set for myself was to get kicked out of school again. And I succeeded.

When my repeated drinking and fighting suspensions hadn't done the trick, I decided to try something extreme. My English teacher, Mr. Burroughs, a sharply dressed gray-haired bastard, had been a member of the Elk's Club with my father. Rather than having sympathy for me, he decided it was best to challenge me, something I didn't appreciate at the time. Maybe he was trying to get through to me, or felt some kind of duty to my father, a friend and fellow educator. But I wasn't going to stand for it. On the rare occasions I actually did turn in my English papers, a terrified Mr. Burroughs would show the principal, who would give it to his secretary, who would run my papers straight to the school psychiatrist. The loudspeaker would beckon me to the psychiatrist's office and the entire school would think I was psycho. Everyone was on edge from the Columbine Massacre and the faculty wanted me out before the school became a bloodbath. When the last paper I ever wrote came back to me from Mr. Burroughs, I did the school a favor.

The red pen marks correcting every other word, red lines crossing out entire sentences, and a red X destroying an entire paragraph made me see blood. I calmly placed my D- on his desk, wound up and punched him in the eye. His glasses went flying in two pieces across the room and he fell off his chair to the floor. The school probably had a pep rally when I was expelled.

After my mother's funeral the childhood authorities tried to force me to live in a foster home, and my psychiatrist wanted me to attend a special school due to my violent past, negative evaluations and frequent blackouts. I wasn't interested in yet another school, so I split town for New York City and nobody made a fuss.

In New York I got a job as a bar-back in the East Village and drank myself silly. My only hobbies were to talk about starting a punk band and write in my journal.

7

I woke up hazy in a field of frost. A herd of mottled cows grazed behind a barbed-wire fence. The crisp smell of early morning air mixed with manure. No one was out except for me, the cows, and a family of speckled starlings who braved the Midwestern chill. My fingers were pale blue and trembling; I rubbed my hands together and frantically searched for the Lincoln.

After walking through the grass, I found the Lincoln parked one hundred yards ahead on the side of the road. My body felt strange and not just from the cold. It was as if I wasn't myself. Memories of a nightmare flooded back with an intensity I hadn't felt in years. I was sleeping in the back of the Lincoln. My left hand began to pull the tips of my fingers like a glove, stretching them out one by one. The bones of my right hand slid back through my skin, while my left hand held the empty shell of my right hand. I felt my bones slide out of the skin like it was a shirt sleeve. Gliding across my chest, under the skin, creating separation, my hand slid into my left arm pit, widening the hole so my left arm could slip up and out. Both hands now pushed, running under my skin through my chest, past the sternum, up the flesh of my neck, over the rippling larynx and past the ridge of my chin. My fingers poked through the pink gums, ripping them from the jaw bone, and came out of my mouth. Grabbing hold of my lips, pulling back, creating a wider hole, I felt the sharp pain of skin pulling off the bone as my head shifted down inside my scalp. The crown of my head squeezed through my mouth hole like a woman giving birth to a child. My skull escaped from the skin, pushing the shoulders through until a warm pile of wrinkled flesh passed my waist dropping to the bones of my feet on the backseat of the Lincoln. My skeleton was free and set off into the Missouri night.

The Lincoln was parked on the shoulder of a rural road somewhere in Missouri with the back door open and the car light still on. During the night, I must have gotten weary and pulled off the highway to sleep. When the nightmare struck I reacted predictably, by running, a failed attempt to escape the events in my head. Or maybe I was trying to keep up with my fleeing skeleton. I prayed that the battery in the Lincoln wasn't dead. I turned the ignition, and the engine sputtered and fired up and I immediately cranked the heat. As I sat in the driver's seat nothing felt right. My skin was too tight, or maybe my bones were too big. My neck felt longer than before, my shoulders broader. It was as if my skeleton had escaped, and another one, wandering the night, found my empty skin and slid inside like a hermit crab.

Driving through the flatlands of Missouri, passing long stretches of unoccupied territory, I came to understand what the expression "Big Sky Country" meant. I'd never been this far west. There were no buildings, mountains or trees to block the view, just flat land and gray sky that stretched forever. I was an hour or so from Kansas City when I pulled onto I-35 South. Why did I feel so odd? Had that cop in Minneapolis escaped or called for help? Was there a convoy of police and state troopers scouring the area for public enemy number one? Every car in my rearview mirror contained a suspect and every police car on the side of the highway sent my heart to the pit of my stomach.

What happened to my brother?

What happened to those three days of my life?

Were the cops following me?

The radio antenna sternly refused to come out and play. Six months back the Lincoln was broken into and my box of tapes was stolen. Who would steal cassette tapes? I found them all smashed to pieces a block away. Iron Maiden's "Killers," which was buried deep in the glove compartment, between the road maps and the ice scraper, was the only one that survived.

I was sick to death of the tape—and the humming noise that emanated from the rotating wheels as it played. To combat this I had to crank the stereo but even that couldn't distract me from my dark and paranoid thoughts. They haunted me, followed, like angry poltergeists.

Where was my brother?

Were the cops after me?

What happened to me for the past three days?

Why had my nightmares returned?

The silver antenna decided to shoot up and I found a news station. *Four U.S. soldiers died in Iraq as a roadside bombing outside of Baghdad sent the U.S. death total to over 7,000 since the war began. A tornado destroyed several towns in Broward County, Oklahoma. The number of deaths has not yet been confirmed. Unemployment has skyrocketed to 12 percent nationwide. In other news, police and FBI are still searching for 7-year-old Rebecca Moon, who was abducted from a McDonald's parking lot in El Paso, Texas on Sunday March, 1ˢᵗ. The time is now 9:40 A.M. The temperature in Kansas City is 38 degrees.*

I glanced back at Rocky the Vampire Bird-Squirrel who was on the floor in the backseat. Reaching back, I grabbed his neck and pulled him up to ride shotgun. I must have gotten him out of the trunk last night before falling asleep.

Rocky was my favorite possession. And I'd created him. He was a combination of a reticulated gray squirrel and a red-winged black bird. He always kept me company on long trips.

After my parents' accident, I was required to see a psychiatrist to cope with my nightmares and violent behavior. Dr. Lastings Arnold, PhD from Johns Hopkins University, was a lipless, frail man who conjured up images of a ventriloquist's dummy. He had a penchant for red bow ties and hazelnut eyes that never blinked. Dr. Arnold suggested — no, insisted — that I find a hobby or a release for my extreme anger and depression.

"What I believe... you would benefit from most is... to find yourself a type of relaxation pastime," he'd say in his wooden cadence. Then, like a possessed doll, he would turn ever so slightly to his left, to engage me on his sofa. Slowly, he would twist, his body and chair remaining straight forward, tiny legs dangling to the floor, mouth faintly ajar, staring with unblinking eyes, and he would return to speaking.

"A duty that will occupy your mind... distract you... distract you from troubles that bind you. I suggest... no, I insist, that you partake in this type of sedative chore..."

Dr. Arnold suggested chess, building model airplanes or bird watching. I didn't have money to buy model airplanes or a friend to play chess with, but I did have a pair of binoculars. So birds it was.

At first I observed the birds in their natural habitats. I watched them fly, play and perch in trees. They continued on, with no regard for my spying, building their nests, preening one another, singing sweet songs. I paid special attention to the calls that each bird used.

One day I got a book from the library on birds of the Northeast and began collecting different breeds by checking off which ones I'd seen in my notebook. Bluebirds, Blue Jays, Buntings, Cardinals, Chickadees, Creepers, Crossbills, Finches, Grackles, Hummingbirds, Juncos, Martins,

Mockingbirds, Orioles, Robins, Sparrows, Swallows, Tangers, Titmouses, Warblers, Woodpeckers. I observed them all, categorizing the ones I saw in my notebook, the patterns and colors of their feathers, the type of tail, their habits and migration patterns. I also wrote their signature calls phonetically. It got to the point that I'd hear the *peter, peter, peter* of the Tufted Titmouse and know that winter had arrived, or the *cuckoo, cuckoo* of the yellow-billed Cuckoo bird and soon after the rains would fall. I was a bird geek.

When I finally had enough money I bought three parakeets and a small aviary from the local pet store. Besides my mom, they were my only family now that Jim had run off, and I looked after these birds as diligently as I did my mother. Talking to them, cleaning their cage, feeding them a balanced diet, I even gave them spray millet and apple wedges as snacks, and pulled dandelion greens from the backyard to give them as treats. At night I'd place a white sheet over their cage so they could sleep. And during the day I found solace in their singing, preening and the flapping of their wings as they rattled their cage.

One day, when I returned home from school, my little family of birds had all died from what I believed was tainted birdseed. My favorite parakeet, Ozzy, was hardest to part with. He used to dance and chirp wildly when I played the song "Crazy Train." He was, in a strange way, my best friend. I felt an overwhelming attachment. Everything else in my life had died or abandoned me but I wasn't ready to bury Ozzy. In detention Principal Ham, a saggy, red-faced man with fingers the size of hotdogs, made students read library books. I usually read *The Lord of the Rings* but, having finished the series during my many hours of punishment, I searched for something new the next day and came across a book on taxidermy. When I returned from school that night, I measured Ozzy with my mother's fabric tape measure, and cut him open along the breast with my butterfly knife. It felt sickening to peel back my best friend's skin and eviscerate him. Ripping out his tender reddish muscle, tissue and slimy organs with my hands was grotesque, but simultaneously I found it fascinating. Using the measurements, I constructed an identical body to Ozzy's made of wood wool wrapped with scotch tape and twine. After washing and drying his cloak of feathers, I ran plain gray wire through his legs, then wrapped the wire with my father's old pipe cleaners so that the wings would remain full and could be posed into a flying position. Next, I placed my newly prepared innards inside the skin and feathers. Sewing up Ozzy as best I could with very thin fishing wire, I bound his body with string to keep his feathers in place and to allow the skin to dry into position. Ten days later, when I removed the bindings, Ozzy was preserved forever.

Thus began a period of collecting birds and mounting them around my room. I became obsessed with the act of preservation but grew bored with my subjects. Experimenting with different species of animals was the next natural step. The ability to create, to play God and invent my own creatures was how the process of the bird-squirrel evolved.

Rocky was the first species I created on my little Island of Dr. Moreau. I used the normal process to preserve a squirrel. Next, I attached the wings of a dead red-winged black bird I'd found outside. The cool red feathers on the shoulders of its black wings provided Rocky with attitude. This gave me the idea to file his teeth into sharp menacing daggers like a vampire and replace his eyeballs with black marbles. Bored one day, I decided to paint them with crazy red streaks that made Rocky appear even more sinister.

My experiments grew absurd: a pigeon-rat, an attempt to attach a dead cat's head to a crow's body. Rocky was the only one that worked to perfection; he was my masterpiece. And he traveled wherever I went. He wasn't much for conversation, but his presence made me feel more comfortable and not so alone in the world.

I could see the small cluster of skyscrapers that made up downtown Kansas City in the distance. Switching on my signal, I cruised onto the off-ramp while the radio changed from a commercial break into local news.

A rookie police officer in Minneapolis, Terry Conte, remains in a coma.
I turned up the volume.

Conte is in critical condition at Minneapolis General Hospital after being brutally beaten early this morning. He was found handcuffed to a radiator pole in an apartment above his own, after responding to a robbery attempt. The officer suffered internal bleeding in his brain and remains on a respirator. Police thus far have no clues and are searching for the tenants of the apartment, who have not been seen for several days, neighbors say.
I shut off the radio.

"How can he be in a coma?" I said to Rocky. "I only hit him twice!"

"Brutally beaten?" I continued. "He was so much bigger than me."

I turned to Rocky, who just stared off into the distance.

It sounded so horrible. In my mind I'd hit him with the back of my head and punched him in the face when he was on the ground. Knocked out, I believed. A concussion, yes, but a coma, that seemed astonishing. I tried to shake off the feeling of disbelief and guilt, rationalizing the situation.

"He asked for it."

If he'd just heard me out, listened to me, none of this would have happened. Although I despised police officers, I had just wanted to remove myself from the situation, not put the guy in a coma. But I had to do it. He would have arrested me for breaking and entering and drug possession, and who knows what else they'd try to pin on me? The police would now be out in full force searching for me. And if he died, a manhunt would ensue. My only salvation was that he *was* in a coma. At least I didn't have to ditch the Lincoln; he was the only one who could identify it.

8

WEDNESDAY, MARCH 4TH
KANSAS CITY, MISSOURI

---

held the photo of Jim and Charlotte in front of the old store clerk's glasses a second time. He ignored me, his attention fixed on a pile of elastic bands on the counter in front of him. He grabbed one, rubbed it between his fingers, warming the rubber with friction, then stretched it out several times and wrapped it around a basketball-sized rubber band ball he had constructed behind the cash register.

"What do you have in the middle of that ball?" I asked, making conversation, trying to divert his attention from the ball.

"Rubber bands," he snapped. "What ya think I got in there?"

"Well, I thought maybe you started with a golf ball or something."

"Then it wouldn't be a rubber band ball, would it?"

He looked up at me, annoyed. "It'd be a golf ball, wrapped in rubber bands." His eyes rose above his glasses as he peered at me. The glasses slid to the end of his nose.

A few straggly white hairs hung on for dear life between blotches of liver spots and scabs on his bald head. Patches of white hair peeked from the collar of his white v-neck T-shirt. A skin-colored hearing aid wrapped around his right ear and a black cord led to a box hitched to his belt.

I pushed the picture in front of him. He shoved it away, shouting, "I said no! Ain't ever seen him before."

Then he paused, spit a stream of tobacco into a can, and asked, "You deaf or somethin'?"

"I'm not the one with a hearing aid," I pointed out.

"Maybe you're deaf *and* dumb. 'Taint no hearin' aid, it's a radio, see." He moved his hip over and showed me the black box on his belt. I saw the face with a dial and the numbers on it for stations.

"Sorry… my brother, he's missing, so I just wanted to know if he or his wife had come in here?"

"Never seen him. You're familiar-lookin' though. You been in here before?"

"No, I meant has *he* been here?" I repeated, raising my voice a few decibels and holding up the picture.

"You on drugs, missy?" He squinted, "I ain't ever seen him before. Now git out my store!" A few drips of tobacco juice ran down his chin.

"You're senile, old man." I blurted, as he mistook my longer hair for a girl's.

Pangs of hunger began to rumble inside me, I hadn't eaten all day and decided to stop at a tiny barbeque joint called Lil' Jake's in downtown Kansas City. I knew Jim traveled through this town and if he'd have stopped here, I knew they'd remember him.

Jim had a distinctive appearance: long, wavy brown hair with natural blond highlights, big, green eyes and a very feminine bone structure. I never thought we looked related and he was always so much smaller and thinner than I was.

The waiter approached and I showed him the photo of Jim and Charlotte. He told me he'd seen them about a week ago, "They're a real nice couple. The girl didn't eat meat. She didn't eat anything at all, actually. Not even the corn bread or our world-famous Mac and Cheese. She just sat there, quietly."

"Yeah, I think she's vegan," I explained.

"She don't eat no meat or cheese?" he asked shocked.

"Nope."

"I thought maybe she was one of those people who don't eat, uh, bulimic."

"Anorexic," I corrected.

"Oh yeah, one of them." He scratched his head. "I said to her, I said, a girl in your situation's *got* to eat."

"What do you mean, *situation*?" I asked.

"Being pregnant and all."

"She's pregnant? You sure?" I replied, astonished.

"Sure as I know the Royals suck. Her stomach was out to here." He held his hands out way past his waist.

I shook my head in disbelief, running my hand through my hair.

"I know, I know, not eating meat or cheese… if you want a healthy baby, you need to eat like a horse," the waiter replied.

As I made my way through downtown Kansas City, my thoughts stayed on Jim and Charlotte. From what I found on their website, Jim originally went under the name Jim Carnie but changed it to The Carnies after he met Charlotte and she joined the band. Charlotte sang harmonies and played the fiddle while Jim played acoustic guitar and sang. He changed his last name to Carnie after the sordid lot that traveled with carnivals, operating rides and games like the tea cups, the Ferris wheel, ring toss, and so on.

I figured they'd been on tour because that is what they did, after all. They toured the states playing bluegrass, and country music. And they toured extensively. Jim boasted on the website about how many miles he'd traveled over his career, naming their latest album *463,000 Miles*.

I stopped at a few places downtown to question people. A worker at an internet café informed me about the Westport section of Kansas City while I slyly Photoshopped my picture onto the police officer's ID. If needed, I wanted to make sure it looked authentic.

Westport was an artsy neighborhood with an abundance of restaurants, cafés, clubs and live music venues. It wasn't near water so I couldn't understand the name, but it was a charming community nonetheless. The streets were extremely tidy, the sidewalks edged with attractive brick inlays. Lean, curved streetlights lined the road. Globes hung down along the walkway, casting a luminous glow.

I ambled like a tourist taking in the scenery and wondered why Jim didn't live here. Westport was so *him*. At least the "him" that I remembered as a child. The area was quiet and clean. One thing I recalled was how Jim detested litter. As kids, while I played volleyball or swam, Jim used to walk the beaches with a garbage bag in one hand, holding a stick with a nail on the end in the other, picking up trash like he was forced to do community service for some bad deed he'd committed. But he really just hated litter that much.

In Westport people held doors for strangers, ground their own coffee beans, thought making handmade pasta and sharing a bottle of wine with friends would make for a splendid evening at home. Country, jazz, acoustic, rock, metal: the area had a little bit of everything, but I found no evidence that The Carnies had played recently.

The puddle-gray sky threatened rain on my drive from Westport back downtown along Main Street. Clusters of strip malls, gas stations, and scraggly bars clung to the thruway like mushrooms to the base of a tree stump. One of the bars had a gaudy neon sign boasting live music out front, so I swerved into the parking lot.

The Grand Emporium on Main Street was wallpapered in old black and white show bills. Legends like Muddy Waters, B.B. King, Johnny Lee Hooker, Howlin' Wolf and Buddy Guy were joined by Bonnie Raitt, Jon Scofield, and The Smashing Pumpkins. One of those didn't quite fit, I thought.

I grabbed a stool at the bar next to a sallow, unkempt girl with glasses, a messy bun on top of her head, and a Guinness Stout in front of her. She wore a KT Tunstall T-shirt, and brown Gladiator sandals that covered thick black-and-white-striped knee-socks.

Grizzled, greasy, wild hair sprouted from the sides of the bartender's head. His beard was full and fluffy with brown hairs intermittently sneaking through the dominant gray. A prominent jaw gave him an under-bite that slightly slurred his speech.

"The Carnies play here recently?"

"Hmmm… maybe schix months ago," he guessed. "Great band. What can I get ya?"

"Your cheapest beer."

I glanced behind the bar. A sign read: *America, in a word… Freedom.* Above the slogan was a rippling American flag. It was in between the *All Employees Must Wash Hands* sign and the Heimlich maneuver instructions. In one word, how would I describe America?

"You a big fan?" the bartender asked as he placed down a can of Pabst Blue Ribbon.

"Sort of."

"Schit, I really enjoy 'em," he said, shaking his head. "I love blue grass. Their harmonies are tight. And the guitar player's a real picker."

"That's my brother," I said, glancing at the unkempt girl as she fiddled with a flat, turquoise stone that dangled from a chain around her neck.

"Really, he's a sweet guy. Gotta pull his teeth to get a word out of him some days, but when he's on stage, what a performer. It's like he's an entirely different person up there." He nodded to the stage in back. "Personable, funny, outgoing. Why's that?"

"I've never seen him play." I sipped my Pabst.

"Really?" he responded, shocked, like I was missing out on something special.

"We're not very close," I explained, a little sadness and worry creeping into my voice.

The bartender scratched his beard, shifted his prominent jaw. "That's a schame." He shook his greasy head.

"So you haven't seen him in six months?"

"No, he played here schix months ago. But Jimmy schtopped by maybe a week or two ago. He just grabbed a beer and a corndog, his wife didn't eat nuthin' but was big as a house."

I turned and caught the unkempt girl eavesdropping on our conversation, big dimples rippled in her cheeks as she smiled and turned away.

"They say where they were headed?" I asked, wiping the dampness off my sweaty beer can with a napkin.

"Nope, we talked a bit about his new CD and the baby and all." He looked down at the bar, "Gonna be a boy, if you didn't know."

"I didn't," I said, shaking my head.

The bartender set up two shots of Jack.

"Let's schelebrate!" he announced, "To the birth of your nephew."
We clanked glasses.

"Hopefully the kid's a picker like his old man," he said smiling through his beard.

I lifted my shot to my lips, and he warned, "Hey, gotta look me in the eye first or its scheven years bad luck."

The unkempt girl leaned over, touched my arm with her hand, and corrected.

"It's not seven years bad luck," she said, staring into my eyes. "It's seven years bad sex."

"That schure would schuck!" the bartender howled.

And we downed the shots.

9

THURSDAY, MARCH 5TH
WICHITA, KANSAS

A light snowfall dusted the monotonous cornfields as I drove through Kansas. The windshield wipers swept away the accumulating snow. I tried to brush off the anxious feeling that police cars were following me.

The first sign of civilization for hours was the city of Wichita. My bladder began to scream, so I pulled off I-35 to a rest stop gas station. A convoy of eighteen-wheelers was lined up for diesel fuel. I pulled into the self-serve and dropped nearly sixty bucks on 13 gallons of gas. Fucking bullshit. The tank wasn't even full as I parked in the crowded lot and entered the restaurant. After relieving myself, I cut through a line of overweight patrons waiting to fill their orange plastic trays with double cheeseburgers, super-sized fries, and large milkshakes at the Hardee's counter. Illuminated by hundreds of fluorescent lights, a sign dangled from the entrance of the cafeteria reading: Fast Food World.

Stands for Hardee's, Roy Rogers, Arby's, KFC, Not Just Burgers, Taco Bell, Pizza Hut, Papa John's, Dunkin' Doughnuts, Subway, and

Jack in the Box, all surrounded the perimeter of the room. There was no escape. As I tried to flee, cartoon character pitchmen in oversized costumes blocked my path. A giant smiling hamburger, a vanilla shake, and a clown with big red shoes danced and sang, attempting to procure business for their establishments. My mind went to the gun that was tucked into the back of my jeans. The thought of capping a clown or the guy in the hamburger costume made me smirk. Blood would be splattered like ketchup all over the food court. When the costumed freaks realized I wasn't interested they began entertaining a chubby family who sat at a booth. The family filled their pie holes, smiled and laughed. It was like Disneyland for gluttons.

Hitting the convenience store inside the complex, I searched the rack at the counter for a healthy snack. Snickers, Snickers Dark, Milky Way, Milky Way Dark, Three Musketeers, Twix, Twix Peanut Butter, Mars, M&Ms, M&Ms with Peanuts, Hershey's, Hershey's with Almonds, Hershey's White, Reese's Peanut Butter Cups, Almond Joy, Mounds, Chunky, Milk Duds, Peppermint Paddies, Mr. Goodbar, Butterfingers, Baby Ruth, Pay Day, Rolo, Whatchamacallit, Take Five, Whoopers, Skor, Dove Bar, Fifth Avenue, Krackle, Crunch, Heath, 100 Grand, Kit Kat, Snow Caps, Sugar Daddy, Twizzler, Gummy Bears, Sour Patch Kids...

I finally found some granola bars at the end of an aisle, past the potato chips, cheese puffs and Doritos.

No wonder Americans were so obese. The easiest alternative to fast food was cheap junk food, and tons of it. I thought of the poster with the rippling American Flag behind the bar at the Grand Emporium. *America, in a word... Fat.*

Bundled up, I made my way back outside. The sky had become bleached with snow. I lit a smoke, wondering what Stillwater, Oklahoma—my next stop—might have to offer. Thus far, I had proof my brother was in Kansas City a few weeks ago, but it didn't seem like he was there to play music. None of the bars or clubs had The Carnies on any recent show bills. If they weren't playing, what were they doing out this way, especially with Charlotte being pregnant?

The cocaine was the only answer I could come up with. Maybe Jim and Charlotte had something big in the works that forced them to travel south even though they didn't have gigs.

Snow blanketed the parking lot like a bright white field of cotton. For the first time in days my attitude was upbeat. It seemed like I was on the right trail, and as far as I knew, the only person who could identify me to the police was still in a coma. Maybe he'd pulled out of it but had some type of memory loss? I couldn't remember three days of my life, so it was possible, I hoped.

After a few drags off my smoke, I walked through the snow toward the Lincoln. Two stout men, one black and one white, in matching blue jackets approached me. The black guy had pudgy checks, a shaved head, and held a leash that was attached to a large German Shepherd. I noticed fresh paw prints in the snow near the trunk of the Lincoln and my heart stopped for a moment.

The white guy was older and had a mustache. His crew-cut was graying on the sides and his chiseled face reminded me of the actor Tom Skerrit. He held up his hand to stop me in my path and asked, "Where ya headed?"

"Stillwater." I took a drag, sidestepping the dog as it shoved its long nose towards my crotch.

"Why are you going to Stillwater?" the younger black guy questioned as he pulled back the dog.

"What's it to you?" I dropped my cigarette to the snowy ground, heard the hiss of the extinguishing ember, stamped it out with my foot anyway.

"I don't think you should go to Stillwater," the mustache guy announced, as he put his hand in his coat pocket and broke out a police badge.

Before I could get a word out, the black cop with the dog was on top of me, shoving my face against the brick wall of the rest stop. The other bulldog demanded in my ear that I open my wallet.

"How much money are you carrying?" he shouted.

"Whoa, fellas, check my ID," I yelled, as the German Shepherd growled and humped my leg.

"Where's your partner?" the black cop demanded, his face buried in my ear.

The cop with the mustache took out my wallet out of my front pocket and looked through the contents.

"You're a cop?" he said, in a bewildered tone.

"Yeah, asshole," I replied, the side of my face still scraping against the cold brick.

"Why didn't you say so?" he responded.

"You didn't give me a chance." I stepped back from the wall.

"What are you doing in Wichita?" He handed his partner my wallet.

"You're a long way from Minnesota, Officer... Terry Con-tay," the cop with the dog surmised.

"I'm undercover." I turned around, wondering how I was gonna get out of this. "Been working a cross-country drug run from Minneapolis to Stillwater."

I snatched back my wallet from the cop with the dog, gave him a look like I was gonna kill his mother, and put my wallet back in my pocket.

"And you cowboys are jeopardizing over a year's worth of work."

"Ok," the younger cop said apologetically. "I'm officer Pope... Lula here went crazy when we passed your car." He said, petting the dog's head, then nodding to my trunk.

"Celestine," The older cop held out his hand and I shook it. "This area's been hot for a while," he said, as I straightened out my shirt and jacket. "You fit the description of one of the perps we've been waiting for perfectly. When Lula went nuts on your car, well, we assumed you were..."

"I have a trunk full of supply," I snapped before he finished, rubbing the back of my neck where the younger cop clipped me. "I'm on my way to Stillwater to meet with a buyer. Gonna sell him enough blow to bust that fucker for the better part of this century."

"How come we haven't been informed about this cross-country run?" Celestine asked, turning his head slightly, the German Shepherd mimicking his actions.

"*Why* would you?" I snarled, trying to appear tough, like a real cop. "This is a Minneapolis and Stillwater operation, nothing to do with Wichita."

"Well." He was defensive. "If you're coming through *our* territory with shit, it's standard to inform us."

"Ah, they probably didn't want to waste your time." My demeanor switched from tough to embarrassed. "When I started this thing... it was supposed to be Mexicans, illegal aliens, serious drug lords, lots of firearms and cash." I looked at the snow on my shoes. "Turns out, it's just a chemistry major with a clever website and an old high school connection."

"You worked undercover for over a year on that?" Pope cracked.

"Rub it in, asshole," I muttered.

"Why don't they have local take care of it then?" Celestine added, still fishing.

"We did a Jump Street. I was the one who infiltrated the Minnesota connection pretending to be a student at the University. I became friendly with one of the budding chemists and they needed a runner. Everybody else had classes so they asked me to make the transaction. It fell right into my hands." I lit another cigarette, blew a cloud of smoke through the snow flakes. "But we were holdin' out, hoping this thing's bigger than just a few college kids. My Captain's gonna have me for breakfast if I wasted all this time and the department's money on some sophomore cokehead from Eden Prairie."

"You better hope it ain't, man," Pope chuckled. They both had a good laugh at my expense.

"Yeah, well, I'm not making FBI on this collar unless it gets bigger in a hurry." I met eyes with Celestine, "Who's your perp? Maybe we could find a link here between my guys…"

The cop cut me off.

"Hold it right fuckin' there." He held up both hands, warning me to stop. "We put together a huge day and night operation. Word is a large amount of shit is coming through here in the next few weeks." He shifted his head with an arrogant swagger as he spoke, "Some husband and wife team's been working up and down I-35 for at least a year supplying to major towns right under our noses. We're talkin' big-time, a fuckin' career bust that'll put this handsome face on the front page." He pointed to his mug and flashed a cocky cop smile. "We don't have time to hold your hand," he gloated.

"Hey, can't blame me for trying," I said with a smirk.

Their radio began to bark, Celestine whispered something into his partner's ear, and I watched their footprints in the snow as they walked ten feet away to hold a private conversation. Celestine glanced in my direction with a cold, steely glare, doing his best Tom Skerrit impression. He'd probably seen *Top Gun* a hundred times. Guys at his station probably called him Viper. He took out his cell-phone and made a call. I figured he was checking up on me, running my name through police records, my license plate, following procedure. If he gave them Conte's name I was fucked. He closed his phone, said something quietly to his partner, and they walked back over. Celestine came directly at me, but Pope and the dog moved around to my right side. Backed against the brick wall, the parked Lincoln to my left, they had me boxed in. I felt behind me and placed my left hand on the gun handle.

Celestine took a deep breath, putting his right hand in his pocket. The snow began to accumulate on the shoulders of his jacket; his stare was fierce. The dog's eyes focused like I was a giant piece of bacon. Its mouth began to froth. Cold air spat out as he panted.

"OK, Con-tay," he said, pausing briefly. "Hold it right there." He moved in close, I caught a whiff of his cheap cologne. "I hope for your sake you believe in the Lord."

"What?" I was confused.

"Cause you're gonna need it." He put his left hand on my shoulder. I squeezed the gun, my index finger tight on the trigger. "If not." He paused again. "You're gonna be pushing pencils till retirement, ha, ha." He howled, a large cloud of breath filling the air between us. "Ssshit, you spent an *entire year* undercover and all you got is a couple chemistry majors handing out twenty bags at keg parties!"

They both laughed, shaking their heads as they turned to walk off. "Good luck!"

"Fuck yoooou," I responded, shaking my head.

Pope turned after about ten feet as he continued to chuckle. "Call us if you need help corralling a grandma pushing her prescription pain relievers!"

Their laughter faded as they disappeared behind a wall of snowfall. I nearly collapsed from the pent-up tension.

It was a nerve-racking experience, I thought as I climbed into the Lincoln, but fruitful nonetheless. The discovery of Jim and Charlotte's operation by the goon squad meant their drug running was more extravagant than I'd previously entertained. This kernel of information led me to theorize that they may have been in deep with a client or caught the ire of a competitor. Either way, though my search was building slowly, I found solace in the fact that the trail had warmed up. God, I fucking hate cops.

10

THURSDAY, MARCH 5TH
STILLWATER, OKLAHOMA

The day's snowstorm left a graveyard of cars and SUVs along the shoulder of the Oklahoma Interstate. It was a tow truck driver's wet dream. I turned east on Route 51 and passed a sign for the OWPO, Oklahoma White Power Organization. When I arrived in Stillwater the town didn't quite live up to its name. The snowstorm turned into a torrential downpour as the temperature rose in the southern Oklahoma climate. Heavy rains sent me running for a Knight's Inn but, surprisingly, there were no rooms available. The Midwest Businessmen's Association was in town and all the hotels were booked. The hotel lobby was filled with round, red-faced men in suits and expensive watches. Each conversation was about money, business deals, or how to hoard away their money to dodge taxes.

Beatrice, the sweet, frumpy old lady at the front desk put down her Bible and said, "I can always help a person in need." She led me down the hallway to a slightly used double for thirty bucks under the table. "Every fat cat from Norman ta Dallas is here this week. Makes me sick ta see those who got so much waste all their money while others got so little." She sneered as she stuck the thirty bucks in her pocket.

The room was wallpapered to look like a medieval castle. There were big gray stone blocks, arched windows, ivy cascading down the walls, even a painted-on drawbridge. I felt like a serf, but at least I was warm and dry.

Everything in the room was untouched except one of the beds. The comforter was pulled back, revealing wrinkled sheets and ruffled pillows that had fallen to the floor. On the nightstand between the beds was an ashtray overflowing with red, lipstick-stained cigarette butts. Next to that, a little white residue remained in a plastic packet. Under the bed was a forgotten pair of black, high-heeled shoes. Half a joint rested on the edge of the dresser next to the TV.

I stretched out on the unused mattress, my temples throbbing, a dull pain gathered in the back of my skull. Shifting to a fetal position, I felt like someone had popped up from behind one of the towers on the wall and shot me in the head with a crossbow. I rolled over, reached my hand into my knapsack, grabbed a translucent orange bottle of pills and swallowed a painkiller. The intense throbbing settled down after a half-hour and I drifted off to sleep.

When I woke around eleven o'clock at night the rains had subsided. After a much-needed shower, I packed up and decided to search for answers in Stillwater, despite the dizziness of a migraine.

Washington Street, a few blocks from the Oklahoma State campus, was the main strip in town. My brother probably played a lot of gigs here so I stopped at a few places, the first of which was a college bar called the Wormy Dog Saloon. The crowd was young. Hairspray and cleavage were the main accessories for gals. Gents were segregated into two groups, those who dipped Skoal and those who preferred Kodiak. Devoid of spittoons the floor was as difficult to navigate as the icy sidewalks of Minneapolis. The bar had saddles instead of stools.

The bartender checked my ID and warned me in a heavy southwestern accent, "Be careful, nobody come to da Wormy Dog wit' out fallin' off da saddle least one time." He smiled. "An' they ain't city slickers."

The next place I hit was a country bar with music, food and drink. A shrine to Garth Brooks sat above the top-shelf liquor. Apparently he began his career playing in this joint, and they had pictures of him on stage performing. In most of the photos Garth sported a mustache and was a bit heavier than he was now.

At the end of the strip I came across The Copper Penny. The crowd inside was a mixture of co-eds and cowboys, a rare blending of class struggle, between those with educations and those without. Some good old boys shot pool and stared me down like I was a cow breaking from the herd. I spoke to the manager of the bar, Tilly. She was in her mid-forties with the short blond haircut of a twelve year-old boy. I wondered if she was a lesbian, and how that might play out in a straight town like Stillwater. Her face was pudgy and apple-cheeked. She spilled beer down it as she chugged from her mug. She wiped off the excess from her cheeks on the over-sized white Dale Ernhardt Jr. T-shirt she sported.

"The Carnies!" she burped. "Great band, love 'em, book 'em whenever they come through town."

Tilly informed me that she hadn't seen Jim for a while and left me with this advice: "Relax. I'm sure they'll pop up soon enough. Musicians ain't the most responsible people in the world." She pounded the rest of her beer.

On my way back to I-35 I found a random bar advertising live music. Club Blue was dark inside. Dollops of light cascaded from the center of elaborate glass chandeliers. A three-piece band wearing dark, tailored suits and blue neckties played in the back room, on a stage outlined with furls of blue velvet. They stood almost motionless as a spooky, clean rockabilly sound twanged from the amplifiers.

The bar itself was made of thick, dark wood with an expensive baroque design. It smashed my idea of what an Oklahoma bar would look like. It was as if a tornado had swooped up an old New York City hotel bar and dropped it smack in the middle of Nowhere, Oklahoma. The crowd was just as bizarre. A mixture of fashions clashed across the seating area. Eighties, Mod, elegant, working class; flamboyant drag queens surrounded colorful drinks at one table; next to them sat a few well-dressed cowboy businessmen.

Round black tables with electric candles under tiny blue shades occupied the space in front of the stage. A few single men were sprinkled throughout the room of couples. The fattest woman alive was at one table. She had a carpet of curly black hair and wore a sheer, light blue ball gown. In her right hand she held a gold scepter, the left rested on the arm of her wheelchair. With her was a lean man in his late forties with slicked-back hair tucked behind his ears. He wore a bolero tie and light blue blazer with black lapels over a pleated white dress shirt. A pack of Marlboro Reds poked out of his breast pocket. The man's face appeared weathered and cracked, matching his old, tan cowboy boots. It seemed like he'd spent too much time in the powerful southwestern sun, possibly on a chain gang. He stared at me ferociously behind pools of dark eyes and took a drag off a smoke.

I ordered a Johnny Walker Black on the rocks and a beer back. The bartender looked familiar.

The first sign of life on stage came from the lanky bass player, who began to sway with the music. His hair was big and black with tight curls. He must have been around 6'10" with the fro. The singer to his left was handsome and lanky as well, nearly as tall as the bass player. Standing in front of a grand 1950s microphone that mimicked his pompadour hairstyle, he strummed his guitar, every motion precise. Then he plucked a few harmonics and slid his hand up the neck, bending the headstock, making the shrill, clean sound warble through the room. He blended into a quick scale of arpeggios, then back to the wavy harmonics that vibrated off the walls. In the middle of the stage sat the drummer, who had long dark curls coiling over his face. He was all arms and knees, dwarfing his tiny kit. His brushes slapped the snare lightly, keeping an eerily quiet beat behind the surf-like rockabilly. "Six Foot Six" was written in cursive on the kick-plate of the bass drum.

I took a sip of my Johnny Black and noticed the wiry man with the obese woman still hawking me. Smooth scotch filled my mouth, the fumes stinging my nostrils. The bartender stood in front of me. His hair was short and tight like a military man, and his narrow blue eyes stared intensely. I could see him being a sniper, locking in on his target. The name tag on his black vest said: John Wayne.

"You look familiar," I said. "Ever live in New York City?"

"Nope, L.A."

"Were you an actor?" I continued.

"Not really, been in a few… pornographic movies, though." He grinned.

"Wow, congratulations." I held up my drink.

"Thanks." He squinted and walked over to another customer.

I chased the Johnny with a sip of beer and looked around the room. The wiry man continued to burn a hole through me with his beady stare. He looked like trouble surrounded him. Like prison wasn't too far removed.

The couple gave me the creeps, and that uneasy feeling my stomach got when things didn't seem right came upon me.

I wondered if he had anything to do with my brother's disappearance.

"Do you know that guy?" I gestured to the table where the obese woman and the wiry man sat when the bartender returned.

"What guy?" John Wayne responded.

When I turned, they were gone. I looked towards the exit and saw the wiry man wheeling the woman out the door.

A well-dressed gentleman with a brown mustache and a bad black wig held the door and followed them out.

"Right there." I pointed at the front door.

John Wayne glanced up.

"That's Virgil," he said, polishing a glass with a white towel.

"Who is he?"

"Some drifter, he pops in from time to time... never seen the woman before, though. Why, are you interested?" He rose one eyebrow higher than the other.

"Interested in what?" I asked, finishing my beer.

"Table service is for buyers." He nodded to where the couple was sitting before. "They usually pay around a hundred dollars, probably two for you though."

"What are you talking about?" I said, confused.

"You know Club Blue's a swinger's joint, right?" He smirked.

I shook my head, looked at the selection of beer bottles lined up behind the bar and settled on a Lone Star.

PART
TWO
LUST

11

We left the diner and rolled through Main Street, windows down. The radio decided to work and she stretched her tattooed arm and began searching for music. She stopped on a classic rock station that was playing Bad Company's "Shooting Star" and cranked up the stereo.

"I love this song!" she shrieked, singing harmony with the chorus. "Don't you know that you are a shooting star, don't you know?" She pointed at me, either trying to let me know I was a shooting star or to take over the next verse. I turned down the radio.

"You're no fun." She pouted.

Everything in town was one level. This must have been a concession for twisters. Why build a second level when it's just going to get destroyed eventually? We passed a barber shop with a red, white and blue pole out front. American flags hung from every shop in town. It felt like a Fourth of July parade without the fireworks. We rolled by a mom-and-pop pharmacy, the sign swinging on its hinges in the breeze, a butcher shop showcasing large pieces of dead animals in the window, a doctor's office, beauty parlor, the Devil Kill Town Bank, a small grocery store, a gas station crawling with grease monkeys checking the engine of an old Ford truck out front. Everything was Norman Rockwell.

"Not much ta look at?" she said. Opening the glove compartment and fiddling around nervously.

"Any a' this ring a bell, David?" she asked.

"What?" I said, not paying attention, focused on small-town nuances.

"Do you 'member anythin'?" She rephrased.

"I don't even remember your name."

"It's Shawna."

"That's a pretty name."

"Thank you." She smiled.

After a while I glanced over at her.

"What's the deal with all the triangles?"

"I like 'em." She said, fidgeting with the triangles on her necklace.

"Obviously, but why do you like them?"

"You don't member anythin' from last week at all do you?" She said exasperated.

"For the last time, no." I grabbed a cigarette, jammed in the car lighter.

"I told you *all* 'bout my belief in the power a' triangles." She propped her legs underneath her, and kneeled toward me, excited. Her blue and white polka dot dress slid up to expose her long slender thighs.

"The symbol is three perfect lines joined together, equally strong an' balanced, yet it's an odd number, three. You don't usually think odd numbers would create balance."

"Sit back down." I instructed her. "Put your seatbelt on."

"Alright, don't yell." She sat back down, pulled the seatbelt across her chest and scowled at me.

"I didn't yell. Just relax."

"Don't tell me ta relax neither, I hate when boys tell me ta relax." She began angrily inspecting the ends of her hair.

"You're like a child," I spat. We sat in silence for a few moments. I lit my cigarette.

"I'm sorry, so the triangles..." I gestured to her to continue.

"You're not gonna yell at me?"

"No."

"Ok." She got excited again. "So they also represent human beings perfectly."

"How so?" I asked, noticing her pretty smile as I dragged on my smoke.

"Mind, body an' soul, all balanced, evenly distributed, joinin' together in perfect harmony." She made a triangle symbol with her hands, held it to her eye and looked at me through the void.

"Doesn't sound like too many people I know."

"I said, triangles symbolize the harmony a' the mind, body an' soul. It's more a *goal* than a definition." She glanced at me. "They also represent the three points a' personality."

"What are the three points of personality?" I looked at her with a smirk.

"Conscious, subconscious an' the unconscious," she said, counting off each point on her fingers.

"The unconscious? Like being knocked out?" I joked.

"No, like the thoughts an' impulses that control your behavior wit' out you knowin' it."

"That's the subconscious," I informed her.

"They're similar but the subconscious is essentially good. The unconscious is solely bad." She leaned forward to make sure I was paying attention.

"How's it bad?" I blinked.

"Because you don't even realize you're human. The subconscious is driven by your hidden desires. The unconscious is like... possession, driven by your traumatic memories, pain, repression."

We continued east, stretching beyond the center of town.

"Maybe, you aren't balanced proper, an' your unconscious consumed your mind. Maybe that's why you don't 'member nuthin'?" she hypothesized. "Here." She took off one of her necklaces, kissing the triangle emblem and slipped it over my head. "This will help your mem'ry."

"A triangle?" I laughed.

"It's a talisman. They avert evil. Plus I gave it a kiss for luck." She smiled.

"Are you making this shit up?"

"No!" She hit my arm. "It's the truth. You can ask my psychic."

"Sure," I laughed again.

"Think 'bout it. You hear it all the time on talk shows, like *Oprah* or *The View*, even *Montel*." She turned to me. "Folks always wish they could find a balance between their home life, work life, an' still find time for themselves personally. They need ta' utilize the power a' triangles ta' help sort out their lives. Find… synchronicity." She beamed at me.

"Ever heard of pyramid schemes? Those are triangles, right?" I opposed.

"Yeah, my old boss Mr. Bermer at the drug store joined one a' them money-makin' ventures at a conference in Oklahoma City. He lost everythin'. Now he's a nasty drunk." Sadness crept quickly into her voice.

"So much for your precious triangles." I cracked.

"You're not as smart as you think." She grabbed my chin and turned me toward her.

"Cut that out. I'm driving!" I smacked her hand.

"You don't know shit. Triangles can be used for evil as well. Like I was sayin', they're a powerful symbol, for good or bad. Like the star of David?"

"That's evil?" I asked.

"No, it's good, fool." She snapped at me.

"I know, but it's a star."

"No, it's two triangles placed over one another makin' a star. Don't you know anythin'?" She drawled and I ignored her driving east. "Actually, I think it's considered… an octagon is eight-sided. What the fuck is six, a hexagon? Anyway, one triangle points up ta signify fire, the other down for water. An' the center is balance."

"Fine, triangles are the best. They're fucking great."

"I didn't even mention the most powerful triangle a' all."

"Yeah, what's that?"

She began giggling.

"The one between my legs."

12

A fter several miles, Shawna told me to turn left onto a dirt road. It was a bumpy ride so I took it slow, not getting past 15 mph for roughly a half-mile, until we pulled up to a small, faded white cottage.

"Home, sweet home." She got out of the car and slammed the door behind her. I followed.

"This is your place?" I asked, surveying the area. A tree stood in the patchy front yard, a rope tied to it with a tire dangling down. I pictured Shawna swinging on it as a little kid.

"Yeah, well it was my Granddaddy's but when he passed away, I won it. It ain't much but its home. An' it gets me away from my family." She pointed to the tree as she galloped toward the front door. "That's the tire I used ta swing on as a li'l girl."

"You won it?"

"It's a long story." She waved for me to follow her in the house.

She was right. It wasn't much. Her granddaddy built it by hand and that was obvious. Nothing was even. Some of the boards were rotted through. Paint was peeling off the wood. Pale green moss covered the roof. It was an allergy attack waiting to happen. The rusty screen door hung from the hinges, its mesh lining torn. One of the front windows was cracked, and the windowsill below had all but eroded. Inside, the wood floors were warped and buckling, making me feel like I was floating on a boat. Her granddaddy must have been a short man; the ceilings were no higher than seven feet. The living room was cluttered, clothing hanging everywhere. Two sewing machines rested on a long amber wood table.

"That's my baby," she said, pointing to an antique turquoise Singer sewing machine.

Different colored spools of thread lined the table. Various patterns of fabric — frilly white, pink, black doily strips, like on the dress she wore — dangled to the floor. A cup filled with scissors and multi-colored pencils, needles and papers with dress designs were strewn about. Silver tools were placed in a leather belt that stretched across the table, instruments used for fastening sequins and buttons rested next to it. A bald white mannequin stood in the corner, her lips sloppily painted bright red, two pink dots for nipples, a big, black, hairy bush drawn between her legs.

"My brother did that. He's hilarious," she said sarcastically.

Next to the table a headless torso wore a sheer, light green dress with a frilly white lace outline and straps. On a desk beside the table sat a large dollhouse. I peered inside. The rooms were meticulously designed with carpet, wallpaper, mirrors. They were occupied by small dolls dressed in different styles. Some were familiar icons, Marilyn Monroe, JFK, Elvis, Jim Morrison and John Lennon, all done masterfully. A gypsy with a shawl and colorful scarf wrapped around her head sat at a table with a tiny crystal ball in front of her. Her head was twisted backwards. On the other side of the table was a doll that resembled Shawna, with long, auburn hair; she even had little tattoos sewn in her arm and angel wings protruding from her back. To her left was a boy doll who looked startlingly like me.

"My Grammy gave me that dollhouse when I's eight. That's how I started designin'," she said. "Makin' clothes for my precious li'l dolls."

"How many do you have in here?"

"I don't know." She shrugged. "I got a whole bunch over the years. You're a new addition." She smiled at me.

Shawna plopped down on a black sofa detailed in yellow and red flower patterns, edged with gold painted wood.

"I'm tired," she said, letting her arms collapse to her sides, her long auburn hair flowing down to cover her breasts. "Trying ta get through ta you's exhaustin'."

I stood, feeling out the environment.

"Can I get something to drink?"

"Sure, kitchen's over there." She pointed to the other side of the room.

The kitchen was tiny, separated from the living room by cheap, cracked black linoleum tiles at the end of a buckled wood floor. There was a small white stove and a large sink overflowing with dishes. I grabbed a clean glass from the cabinets above the sink and let the water run for a minute before filling it. On my way back to the living room I nearly tripped over an ironing board. Shawna still sat on the sofa, her legs spread wide open the way a child who didn't know any better would sit in a dress. She stared at the blank screen of a small white TV with an antenna on top. The rabbit ears stretched to capacity with pieces of aluminum foil affixed to the tips.

"Why don't you sit down? I have an idea that'll jog your mem'ry."

"Sure, I have a million questions, I don't even know where to begin," I responded.

"That's *not* what I had in mind," she said mischievously, pulling up the polka dot dress to reveal her underwear. They were tiny, navy blue panties with white polka dots and frilly white edges that matched her dress. She ran her fingertips along the white lace edges.

"Do you like them?" she asked.

"They're very you," I said, trying to stay focused on why I was there.

"I made 'em myself."

"I figured." I took a sip of my water. She looked good enough to eat.

"I make lots a' things," she said, giggling. "I'm very talented."

"I can see." I said, looking at all her designs that hung around the room.

"C'mere," she cajoled me, grabbing my hand and pulling me between her legs.

"Wanna see a magic trick?" Her eyes grew wide.

"Sure." I figured I'd humor her.

"Watch." She reached her hand out, rubbing my penis through my jeans. It filled up with blood, grew hard, "See, magic!" She laughed. "I told ya I's talented."

"That's not so hard." I quipped.

"It will be." She giggled again, pleased with her sexual innuendos. She began unbuttoning my pants, simultaneously pulling my underwear down to my ankles.

"See, there it is," she said, tapping at my beauty mark with her index finger.

I leaned in, kissed her red lips. She slid her silky tongue into my mouth briefly. Then she pulled away giggling, lying back on the sofa with her arms above her head, dropping them behind her on the armrest of the sofa, placing herself in a submissive position. I stood in front of her, naked. I felt a little foolish with a full-on erection, but removed my pants. I positioned my body beside hers on the sofa as she began gently rubbing her polka dot panties.

"Do you like my panties? Aren't they ador'ble?" She gasped, losing her breath slightly.

"They're really adorable. Just like you." I smiled. "You're like a grown-up child."

"I'm a precious li'l doll," she mused, letting her hair fall in front of her face.

I watched her put more pressure on her clitoris with her middle fingers. Placing my hand on hers I felt a rush of wetness seep through the fabric of her panties. She released a few small moans of appreciation, brushing the hair from her face, as I placed my mouth over hers gently, sucking tenderly on her soft, fleshy lips, while continuing to massage her little triangle. I ran my finger along the edges, manipulating it like a toy. The more I stroked the wetter she got. Then I slid my fingers down, working her dampening panties deep inside her, saturating the material.

"Ohhh, do you like my panties?" she asked.

I nodded, kissed her again, adjusted my hand to pull down the drenched panties. When I forced her legs apart, spreading them wider, one fell from the sofa to the floor.

Looking down, I saw several spider-veined scars pointing in each direction, surrounding her vagina like a trap.

I slid inside her and it was like nothing I'd ever experienced before. Her pussy felt like jelly. It was as if thousands of tiny tongues were massaging me in every direction the further I penetrated. Moans came from her lips; she squeezed my back tightly as I gently thrust inside her.

"Ohhh, do you like my pussy?" she asked. "Do you?"

"Yes," I whispered, moving my lips inside her ear. "Has anyone ever made you this wet before?"

"No, no baby, ohhh, nobody."

I reached down with my right hand, picking up her soaked panties, rubbing them on her cheek.

"Do you see how wet I get you?" I whispered, still rubbing the soiled panties on her face.

"Oh, my God, YES! Oh, God, YES!" She groaned louder.

I thrust inside her again shocking her shoulders against the cushions of the sofa, moving the panties from her cheek to her mouth and nose, holding them over her face.

"Do you like that?" I asked.

"Ohhhh, fuck yeah! Fuck yeah!" she cried, struggling to get the words out with the wet fabric covering her mouth.

I maneuvered the leg hole of the panty over her lips, forced my tongue into her mouth. The scent of her panties overwhelmed me. I fought the urge to release inside her, pulled my head back, arched my back and began to fuck her harder, as she slid her hand down and began rubbing her clit.

"Fuck, I'm gonna cum baby, fuck, ohhh God! I'm gonna cum, fuck…" she cried.

I pushed her panties into her mouth, continuing to slide deep inside her, flexing, expanding and contracting, as I plunged. She groaned in delight with each swell, rubbing herself faster and harder. Holding the drenched panties in her mouth, pushing more fabric in with the tips of my fingers, the scent of her pussy lingered on my face. Her juice and my sweat mixed together, running down my face. I felt her body begin to quiver beneath me, her legs shaking. I gave her a rapid series of powerful drives before releasing deep inside her, fucking her harder and faster and harder. She squeezed me tight and let out a succession of thunderous moans.

Her body went limp. Her arms collapsed, one fell off the couch, her knuckles scraping the floor. I kneeled above her. Her eyes were closed. She breathed heavily, her chest pounding, the little polka dot panties still bunched up and dangling from her mouth.

13

FRIDAY, MARCH 6TH
DEVIL KILL, OKLAHOMA

"So tell me, how'd we meet?" I asked. Shawna walked through the kitchen wearing only a black robe with a colorful, wiry dragon pattern embroidered on the back. I sat on the sofa and put my T-shirt on.

"You were alone." She walked over, handed me my glass of water, then snuggled next to me. "Covered, I mean completely covered in dirt, watchin' TV in this bar up the road. I's havin' a drink by myself, I actually hate that place an' never ever go there."

She grabbed my pack of cigarettes off the coffee table and lit one.

"You was sittin' next ta' me at the bar an' ordered a beer. I felt sorry for you so I asked if you'd had a hard day's work."

"What'd I say?" I asked.

"You told me you rolled your car an' got thrown into a ditch." She laughed.

"Did you believe me?" I sipped my water.

"No, you didn't have no cuts or bruises or broken bones or nuthin'. You's just filthy. So I said what really happened? An' you told me your dog died an' you buried him… then I said you musta had a pretty big dog?"

She handed me the cigarette.

"What happened next?" I took a drag, watched the tendrils of smoke rise through the air and bounce off the low ceiling.

"You said that I was the prettiest girl you'd ever laid eyes on. I don't know why, but you looked all sexy covered in dirt. It turned me on serious." She laughed.

"You're a very strange girl."

"Everybody says that." I stabbed out the cigarette in an ashtray on the coffee table. Her robe slipped open to reveal her nakedness.

"No panties," I flirted.

"No." She laughed. "I gotta' do laundry."

"It was the truth, by the way."

"What?"

"You are the prettiest girl I've ever seen."

We fucked again on the sofa.

Later, Shawna made some baked beans and walked out of the kitchen holding an old silver pot.

"It's all I got here. I really need ta go grocery shoppin'," she said as she poured the beans into two bowls on the table. She handed me a fork and sat beside me.

"Do you 'member when we was lyin' in bed an' I told you your teeth reminded me a' Patricia Arquette?" she asked smiling, raising her single eyebrow.

"Nope."

"Yeah, you got that cute li'l snaggle tooth that juts out right there." She pointed, almost touching my crooked tooth. "Just like Alabama in *True Romance*. Alabama, that's where I's born?" She looked in my eyes. "Any a' that sound familiar?"

"No… so why was I really covered in dirt?" I wondered.

"You never told me. Well, you never told me the truth."

"What happened next?" I grabbed the salt and dashed some on the beans.

"We went ta the diner, got a bite ta eat, came back here, you showered an' we made mad love all night long." She glowed. "I can't believe you don't 'member that? Nearly set the bed afire."

"Sorry." I gulped down some of the beans. The salt made them palatable.

"What else can you tell me?" I kept quizzing her.

"Not much, you said you had ta split town for a while but that you'd come back if you trusted me. Then we drank a few bottles of wine an' you shaved off my eyebrow. God, I must've been blind drunk ta let ya do that." She shook her head, embarrassed.

"What about the coke? In the diner you said you knew I had it."

"Oh yeah." She moved her hair from her face. "You said someone you knew was a pusher an' owed you a bunch a' money. So you was gonna drive ta Minneapolis an' pick it up so we could sell it an' make money," she said nonchalantly.

"And you didn't care that I was going to sell coke?" I asked.

"Nah, you said you hate that stuff, but it was the only way you could get back the money your friend owed you." She took a mouthful of beans and continued talking as she chewed. "We needed money... ta start our lives together, so I thought it was as decent an idea as any."

"What happened next?" I prodded her, polishing off my beans.

"I don't know... oh, yeah, when I woke up the next mornin' you was gone," she said. "Part a me, naturally, never thought I'd see you again. But you left the sweetest note tellin' me where an' when ta meet."

"Do you still have it?" I asked.

"Course." Shawna left the room and returned with a piece of paper.

The note was in my handwriting.

To the prettiest girl I've ever seen,

This was the best night of my life. I've never met anyone like you or felt this way before. I'm sorry that I have to leave but I promise I'll return! Meet me at The Railway Diner at the back table in the corner on Friday at noon. As

I write this, I can still taste your pussy on my lips. I don't think I'll wash my face for a week. You're amazing!

I love you!

David

I sat quietly for a while. A headache began to form again.

"You ok sweetie?" She paused. I didn't answer her, hoping the pain would pass.

She put her arms around me, kissed me.

"Let's go ta bed, honey." She grabbed my hand and stood up.

"In a minute."

She bent over, kissed me on the forehead, twirled and dropped her robe to the floor. As she walked away with that sexy little wiggle I noticed she had black angel wings tattooed on her shoulder blades. My eyes moved down to her smooth ass as she swayed out of the room. I started to get hard again.

She almost made my headache go away, but the thoughts of my brother returned and my desperation was growing. Shawna didn't have any information for me because I never told her anything. All I got from her, if she was to be believed, was that I was here a week before for a wild night and did some strange things. I could only remember waking up freezing in the back of the Lincoln in Minneapolis. That's what I could definitively prove to myself. Fact: I was in Minneapolis and drove to this small town.

I took my last Tramadol, chased it with water, thought about Shawna. She was an angel. We'd only known each other six hours, at least I only remembered knowing her six hours, but why I'd told her I loved her and why I'd returned were easy to figure out. It was hard to remain focused on my search with her so close by, knowing that luscious body waited for me in the other room. Her scent lingered in the air, indulging me to follow.

I shook off her charms, got out my notebook and began writing.

Where is my brother? Why was I covered in dirt? How did I get here and why did I return? What happened to make me lose three days?

A cheap jug of red wine sat on a rickety green table in the kitchen. The wine tasted like shit, but it helped accelerate the pill's effect. I put down the jug and opened the large drawer in the table. Inside was a corkscrew, some large serving utensils, a couple of screwdrivers, a hammer, little knickknacks and a pair of brass knuckles. I took out the brass knuckles, put them on my hand and made a fist. Why did she have them? Maybe girls in small towns needed to protect themselves, too. I took them off and slid them into the back pocket of my jeans, thinking they might come in handy sometime. Moving to the living room, I began a list in my notebook of things to do the next day. I needed structure. My search was too chaotic, unfocused. Everybody remembers strangers in small towns. I considered the places I would've stopped. It was a short list: bars, anywhere cigarettes were sold, motels, all had to be checked. Maybe one of these yokels would help me remember? Under the list I wrote, *Get more pills!*

A strange feeling twisted inside me. Had I done something horrible? Had I hurt anyone? This entire trip has been so bizarre. And the return of my migraines and nightmares frightened me. I didn't feel comfortable in my skin.

Flipping through the pages, trying to find a note or clue, I came to a drawing of a strange tree. It looked as old as the earth, slanted, with odd limbs coiling out in unnatural directions. This particular tree would have a history, a story, a personality all its own. Located somewhere sacred or cursed, like an Indian burial ground.

I walked into the bedroom. Shawna lay in bed peacefully, beautifully, relaxed. She looked like a small kitten, curled into a ball, contorting her spine in a way that didn't seem humanly possible. She was wrapped in all that long auburn hair, and a wooly Afghan blanket. When I lay down and placed my arms around her thin body, she turned. Burying her head in my chest, she looked up at me.

"You need ta trim your nostril hairs."

"Shut up," I said smiling, covering my nose self-consciously with my hand. I began tracing the tattoo on her shoulder, circling the antique frame with my finger tips, outlining the little child inside with the red lips.

"Last Friday?" She tilted her head, resting it on my chest. "Do you even 'member sayin' you loved me?"

"No, I'm sorry, it's all blank," I said, stroking her head like a cat.

"I like that," she purred.

"If I scratch you behind the ear, will your leg start to shake uncontrollably?"

"I'm not a dog," she whined.

"You're not?" I inspected the ends of her hair. "Looks like I should start mixing some raw egg into your food. It'll give you a nice shiny coat," I teased her. "You're a good girl, aren't you?" I scratched her scalp behind the ear.

"Stop it," she said playfully, giving me a peck on the chest. "Go ta sleep, baby."

I pulled her face next to mine, kissed her. She nestled her head in the curve of my neck. Her hair smelled like flowers. I planted a kiss where the hair parted on her head, closed my eyes and tightened my embrace. That moment I experienced something I hadn't felt in more than ten years. I had forgotten what it was like to care for someone other than myself. I put one hand on her hip, slid the other down and began rubbing her pussy. She made sinful little moans, reached back with both hands and grabbed the bars of the headboard. Her eyes closed, she bit her bottom lip and her chest began to pound.

14

I awoke exhausted, drenched in sweat from my paranoia of the unknown. Shawna, still soundly asleep, entwined my body as if we were one entity. I snaked free from her grasp without disturbing her deep sleep and decided to head into Devil Kill, letting her rest. My shaking, sweaty hands made it difficult to write but I left a sweet note on the coffee table with my phone number at the bottom. The search for Jim and his wife was still urgent, but my most pressing need at the moment was to refill my prescription. Anxiety was taking hold and without pills, I wouldn't be myself.

The prairie seemed to stretch forever. Day had broken and the sun burned off the early morning dew, sending moisture into the air. A hazy fog above the earth carried for a few miles toward the small town. With the windows down, the warm breeze felt like spring. The change in climate was drastic compared to Minneapolis. Nearly a thousand miles south meant roughly a sixty-degree difference in temperature. Six degrees for every hundred miles.

Devil Kill was a throw-back to another era. There were no big-name stores or chain restaurants; all the businesses were family-owned. The working-class community still clung to old traditions and the heavy hand of Christianity. It would be more appropriate to view this place in black and white.

I eased into a parking spot between two pickup trucks. They both had bumper stickers of American flags, one reading, "Support your local Union," the words circling around two crossed hammers. The other bore the slogan, "My other ride's a Harley." As I walked along the main strip, a tan smell-hound tied to a gun rack in back of an old truck woofed at me. I entered the brightly lit bank foyer and a large man in his late thirties, nostrils flared, his bullish face crunched under a shag of black hair, came toward me. Most of his left hand was missing. Stumps of flesh and mangled knuckle hung from the cuff of his blood-speckled, light blue jumpsuit. The patch on his chest read: Sawyer. He made a point to bump into me as he exited the bank.

"Bitch!" he yelled in my ear, his breath awash with alcohol.

I stared back at him, my anger rising.

"You got a fuckin' problem?" He wiped his runny nose with his blood-stained shirt sleeve. I continued onto a bank machine, not wanting trouble.

"That's what I thought... asshole!" He called back, stumbling to the sidewalk.

He was wasted, handicapped, and most likely out of his mind. Plus the mean-looking bastard was twice my size. Grinding my teeth, I fingered the gun in my jacket pocket and thought about making him beg for his life in the street. Instead, I went to the bank machine, got some quick cash, and tried to shake off my rage. But I couldn't. Taking my right hand I slammed it down on the screen of the bank machine and shattered the glass. The further I traveled, the harder it was to keep my anger in check.

The bell on the town church rang eleven times as I ambled down the sidewalk. I found a doctor's office nestled between the fresh-baked aroma of Farrar's bakery and Tweedy's Hardware store.

Lemon Pine-sol scented the small, gray-carpeted office. Hunting, fishing, sports and medical magazines fanned across a russet-colored coffee table. The tranquil sounds of a small rock-waterfall tumbled next to a large, bubbling fish tank. Several red and white tropical fish flapped their gills and looked out with the long, sad expressions of prisoners. A poster of the human body hung on the wall with lines pointing to the major organs. That's where my gallbladder was. I sat on a plush, leather sofa and filled out paperwork using a phony name. A plump, buttoned-up mother hugged the blue purse on her lap and smiled politely as our eyes met. The small pink jacket next to her had *Sarah* written on it in white, cursive stitching. The blue-haired receptionist called my name in a Midwest accent thick enough to churn butter. She walked me to the hallway and told me to wait in the first room on the right.

Either I misunderstood her drawl or she made a mistake because I opened the wrong door. A slice of light from the hallway pierced the dark room, illuminating a well-dressed older gentleman with a stethoscope and a naked child with ribbons in her hair. I heard light moaning, and crinkling of the sanitary paper on the patient's cushioned seat.

"W... what in the world!" the man's startled voice called from the dark.

"Sorry, wrong room," I blurted, shutting the door quickly. Walking nervously down the hall to an open room, I entered and stood before a sizeable mahogany desk. On the wall behind it was an arrangement of pictures. A white-haired, well-dressed man dominated the display. I assumed he was the man I'd walked in on. There were smiling photos of children, grandchildren, the doctor and his silver-haired wife. In one picture the doctor shook hands with another important-looking man. They smiled into the camera on a stage, an American flag in the background. A series of diplomas hung next to the pictures as well as a framed letter from Dwight D. Eisenhower, congratulating him on his recent marriage, dated 1964 and stamped with an official presidential seal. The shelves on the wall were filled with medical books and journals. On the top shelf were a number of awards and trophies.

The doctor entered the room quickly. He was a short, proud man with a pristine appearance. The part in his hair was straight as an arrow, not a single white hair out of place. His light gray suit was pressed and tailored to fit. A large jewel-encrusted gold watch sparkled under the office lights like a mirrored ball.

"Hello, hello, how are *we* today?" he said, smiling.

"Not bad."

"I see you are admiring my awards." He smiled.

I looked at him, nodded and then looked back at a heart-shaped statue from the Children's Hospital for his sustained excellence in pediatric medicine.

"You do something for forty years and you're bound to get an award for it. Please, sit." He motioned to the chairs in front of his desk. "What can I do for you?"

"I'm from New York, my car broke down on the way to Austin, and I happen to be out of my medication. So I wanted to get a prescription while I'm waiting for the repairs." I made a writing gesture like I was asking for the check at a restaurant. He gazed at me whimsically.

"That's terrible. You know what they say, bad things happen to good people." He held out his hand, "My name is Dr. Pepper."

"Are you serious?" I cracked, shaking his hand, noticing his gleaming cufflinks.

"Completely," he snapped, pulling his hand back.

"You're named after a soda?" I chuckled.

"I assure you, I have no relation to that particular brand of carbonated beverage." He smiled, enunciating every word. "Wish I did... I'd be a rich man." He got up and sat in the chair next to me.

"I'm sorry Doc, but uh, could you help me out? I get headaches and they're becoming unbearable."

"I'm sure we can work out something," he said, placing his hand on my knee.

"Uh, thanks doc," I said, waiting for him to remove his hand.

"So, do you have much money?" he asked in a sympathetic voice as he inspected my beat-up shoes and ripped jeans.

"Not much. Like I said, my car broke down and most of my money's going to repairs," I lied.

"Well, that is terrible." His hand still rested on my knee. His smile grew broader. "You'll find that Midwestern hospitality is a requirement here in Devil Kill."

"That's great, 'cause my vision's blurry, making it difficult to drive and I have to be in Austin tomorrow for work," I said, shifting my leg, trying to get his hand off.

"That's very troubling," he stated, overly concerned. "You are in a desperate situation." He slid his hand up my thigh.

"Whoa!" I said, startled, as his hand inched closer to my crotch and squeezed.

"Don't worry. I have the answer to all your problems." I slapped his hand away.

"Doc, cut the shit!" I moved back in my chair.

"You don't want your pills?" He feigned concern, pulling his hand back slowly.

"Not that bad," I snapped, shifting my chair away from him.

He gazed to the ceiling in contemplation. "An addict will do most anything for their habit." His thin lips sucked in as he shook his head side to side. "I *have* learned that over the last forty years."

"I'm no addict," I replied.

"Hmm, the dark circles." He gestured to my eyes, "The trembling hands, cold sweats?" he diagnosed. His grin straightened to a more serious expression.

"Doc, I'm no addict." I removed my wallet from the back pocket of my jeans, flipping it open to reveal the police badge. "I'm a cop."

"Dear me." A shade of embarrassed pink painted his cheeks.

"I should arrest you for solicitation, among other things, but you might actually enjoy prison," I cracked.

"Wha-, what-a, can I do for you officer?" He stuttered. His hands trembled as they touched his shocked lips. "I hope you didn't misunderstand, my, my concern…"

I cut him off. "Just write up a prescription for Vicodin and Tramadol, perv, with refills," I ordered.

"Yes, officer. No, no problems there." He laughed, nervously as he stood up and made his way around the desk.

I propped up my feet on the desk. He looked at them, then rifled through his drawer for a pen.

"Sooooo, your name's really Dr. Pepper?" I picked up the triangular name plate off his desk.

"Yes… my, my whole life, ha, ha, yes, yes, well, most of my life anyway, wasn't born a doctor, you know," he said, anxiously searching for his medical pad under the papers on his desk.

"That's fucking ridiculous," I said. His eyes rose to mine and quickly shifted back to his pad. "What asshole would become a doctor with the last name Pepper?"

"Oh, I don't know. I guess I should have thought about my profession more thoroughly," he replied anxiously.

"You really are a fucking idiot aren't you?"

"Yes, yes I am," he said, handing me the prescriptions in his shaking hand. "Now please… leave."

"Say it." I took the papers, checked to make sure they were correct.

"Say what?" he asked.

"Say, my name is Dr. Pepper and I'm a complete fucking idiot."

"Are, are you serious?" he asked, nervous, not making eye contact, loosening the knot in his tie.

"Completely."

"You've got your prescription, now please leave," he begged.

"Say it, Doc." I pulled the gun from my jacket pocket, walked around his desk and pointed the barrel at his temple.

"Oh, dear!" He began to sob. "P... please, please don't." He shielded his eyes with his hand.

"Say it." I said calmly, pressing the gun hard through his hands into his temple, making an indentation in his skin. Sweat formed on the brow below his perfect white hair, dripping down his forehead as he shook.

"I know what you're up to in the examining room, Doc, and it's gonna end right here and right now." I jammed the gun as hard as I could into his temple ripping his skin. Some blood ran down, mixing with his tears, catching in the cracks of his deep crow's feet as I began to fill with rage.

"Now say it!"

"M,m,m, my, my name is Dr. Pepper and I'm, uh, uh, complete... fu... fuck... fuck...ing, fucking idiot."

15

SATURDAY, MARCH 7TH
DEVIL KILL, OKLAHOMA

Further along into scenic Devil Kill, I came across a seedy log tavern decomposing on a hill called The Slaughtered Cow. Thoughts of my brother, the screams on the voicemail and my terrible sleep habits were getting the best of me. A cold beer would facilitate the pain killer I'd just popped and settle my nerves, so I decided to stop.

The hearty stench of urine converged with that of overcooked meat. The smell was infused in the old bristling wood floors of what must've been the dirtiest bar in America. A white rotating plastic fan blew smoke and the stink around the bar. Mismatched chairs—wooden dining, metal folding, plastic leisure—circled wobbly tables. An army of dead flies were glued to the dirty beige tangles of tape that spiraled down from the ceiling.

This was how I'd imagined the Old West. Some time in the 1800s, Devil Kill was a shanty town, built purely for the railroad crew that was working its way west. They'd need a place to get liquored up at night, and this was it. Whisky bottles with XXX across the front, a player piano for entertainment and, of course, a bearded drunk who could speak only in gibberish.

I found the epicenter of the hideous odor in the bathroom — a breeding ground for disease. Pandora's box. Lining the wall was a silver metal trough with an old, green garden hose affixed to the top running along the seam where two logs came together. Holes were poked in the side of the hose and drops of water made pinging sounds as they hit the trough's metal bottom. Indoor plumbing must have been a newfangled invention here in Devil Kill. I held my breath and made sure not to come in contact with anything.

On my way to the bar I saw Sawyer, the one-handed man who'd confronted me in the bank, sitting at a table full of beer bottles. Four surly characters, all dressed alike, uniforms splattered in blood, joined him. They were cussing and cracking up about something.

Perched on a stool at the bar sat a very old woman. Her hands rested beside a short glass of beer on a coaster. She held a wadded-up white handkerchief in one. Broad black sunglasses shielded her eyes and long rivers of skin ran down her droopy, brown-speckled cheeks. Strands of white spun from a spool on the top of her head. A lavender cardigan covered her hunched shoulders, and a shapeless, teal floral sundress dangled to her box-shoed feet. Beside her, a white Labrador Retriever, graying around the eyes, with a thick, brown harness attached to its back lazily lapped water from a silver metal bowl on the floor, spilling it and soaking its own paws. The woman could have been one hundred years old, as I sat down next to her at the bar and ordered the shot-and-beer special, Old Crow and a Lone Star for $3.50.

"Don't sound like yer from 'round these parts," the elderly woman said in a slow, heavy twang.

"I'm from New York."

"City?" Her voice raised an octave.

"Yep."

"You Jewish?" Her voice climbed again.

"Nope."

"You can stay then." She nodded. "Don't want no Jew wanderin' in when I's havin' my three o'clock drink. Three o'clock's the hour a Christ's death ya know," she informed.

Her words slurred together. To completely understand her I needed to focus on her mouth like I was reading lips. "The Jews kilt Christ, ya know."

"I don't. I'm not very religious," I replied, taking my beer from the bartender.

"Most young folk don't care, but nearly every day fir the last seventy years I've a drink 'ere ta toast Jesus. You could say it's my job. Ta' let atheists know who died fir their sins." She turned her head to face me, but glanced up to the ceiling as she held out her tiny blue veined hand. "My name's Prudence."

I shook it gently for fear her cold hand would crumble to dust if I held it too tight.

"This here's Roscoe." She pointed to the white dog on the floor. "He's an excitable one."

I looked down and Roscoe yawned, his long tongue stretched out as he coughed.

"He ain't much fir conversation, but better 'an most people I drink wit." She grinned.

I nodded, turned to my shot of Crow and downed it.

"Don't get too many Yankees 'ere in Devil Kill," she said, dabbing her wet lips with the handkerchief. Her slurred speech made an uncomfortable amount of saliva draw in the corners of her mouth. Or perhaps the amount of saliva was what slurred her speech. Either way, it wasn't pleasant.

"I'm just passing through town," I said, washing down the liquor with a swig of Lone Star.

"That's the way we like it 'round 'ere. You know everybody an' everybody know you," she stated firmly. Was I about to get run out of town by the oldest bully in history?

I glanced around quickly, tapping the bar like a drum as she turned to me again.

"Devil Kill's been kind ta strangers, though. Ever since the late eighteen seventies when Reverend Cornelius Hitchcock founded this town."

I wanted to ask if she was here for the ground-breaking. Instead, I sipped my beer and rearranged the wording in my head.

"Did you know him?"

"Yes... he was an incredible man. Very close ta God an' a handsome, charismatic man. He was one a' the first travelin' evangelists a' the south." She smiled. "Reverend Hitchcock settled 'ere in Devil Kill from Kentucky wit' his disciples after the war. Before Oklahoma was even an official state a' the union. It was Injun territory an' they the ones who name it Oklahoma. Ya know what it means?"

"Oklahoma," I replied. She nodded. "No?" I examined the sagging folds of skin under her chin, wondering if I would have the same one day.

"It means *red people*." Prudence turned, feeling the bar with her hands as she moved. "The Choctaw name it hopin' Oklahoma'd be a separate Injun state. But God told Reverend Hitchcock he should come ta this territory an' spread his word."

"Wasn't that dangerous?" I asked, petting the dog as he stood up and began sniffing my pant leg. "Coming to an unoccupied territory?"

"Oh my, yes. The Injuns was angry Godless peoples, they didn't want no whites on their settlement, an' this was long b'fore the land grab a '89." She felt around on the bar top for her glass. I tried to help her by pushing the glass and she snapped, "Don't help me! I been makin' my way fir da last fifteen years wit' out sight an' help from no one 'cept Roscoe... don't need no help now."

"Sorry." I sat back a bit.

"I'm a proud old woman, you know. Oldest in Devil Kill." She smiled.

"I can see," I said, as she got a hold of her glass, shifting it in front of her.

"Reverend Hitchcock was a brave, brave man," she continued. "He come out here sooner than allowed an' founded Devil Kill. That's how the name Sooner's come about. Because Reverend Hitchcock come out ta' Oklahoma *sooner* than whites was allowed." She gurgled, began coughing into her white handkerchief, and then composed herself.

"Excuse me," she said politely, dabbing the frothy corners of her mouth.

"So, why's the town called Devil Kill?"

"Reverend Hitchcock originally named the town Paradise, Oklahoma. But in the spring a '81, an angry beast a' the devil come upon the town. Fearlessly, Cornelius did battle wit' the demon an' smote him down wit' the fury a' God!" Her hands trembled as she explained the origin of the town's name. Her mouth filled with phlegm, slurring her speech even more. "Word spread 'bout his battle wit the beast an' more come ta follow the Reverend an' listen ta God through his word."

"What was the beast?" I became fascinated by her story.

She began to smirk. "From what I's told. Wasn't there ya know. I ain't *that* old." She chuckled, wiping spittle off her chin with the handkerchief. "The beast a' the devil was *believed* ta be a two-headed buffalo."

I smiled, took a long swig off my beer, brought my head down. Prudence felt around for her drink, her head in the clouds. Roscoe returned his graying face to the floor in front of his bowl.

"What happened to the Reverend?"

"The Reverend passed away from pneumonia in 1920 when I's six years old. Wit' Cornelius Hitchcock buried, still pious as ever, Devil Kill will always be devout," she said as sorrow filled her voice. "But the world move fast at that time… toward the future." She held her beer glass with both hands. "The slaughterhouse become the town's major source a' economy an' wit' it, people begun ta care more 'bout themselves an' money than history."

Nodding along with her sentiment, I rose from my stool.

"Thank you," I said.

"Enjoy your stay." She smiled, her saggy cheeks wiggled from the bones of her face. "Not many towns left in America wit' the charm a Devil Kill."

As I left, Sawyer stared at me. I looked away, heading for the exit.

"Hey bitch!" he called, showing all the charm Devil Kill had to offer. "Get the fuck outta my bar!"

The boys at his table cackled and patted him on the back. I continued towards the door silent on the outside, but my anger growled inside with each step I took. I counted backwards from ten, an anger management technique a psychiatrist taught me years ago that didn't work then and didn't work now. Rage swelled within me. I bit my tongue, feeling like a coward for not sticking up for myself. Their laughter was like a cold slap in the face. I fought the urge to take the gun out of my pocket, kick open the bar door and get Wild West on Sawyer's entire table. Fifteen bullets in the clip would probably take out half the inbred population of Devil Kill. It would fix this charming town for good. I'd start with that one-handed asshole and finish with Dr. StrangeLove back in town. I spit on the ground, kicked over a metal garbage can and watched as the lid rolled down the hill, clanging and spiraling to a stop.

16

I picked up Shawna at her shack. She'd agreed to give me a tour of Devil Kill if I dropped her off at the laundromat afterwards. Her hair was in pigtails, her body wrapped in a pink baby doll outfit. I loaded a large bag of dirty laundry into the back of the Lincoln. White ruffles on the edges of Shawna's dress gave it the appearance of oversized lingerie or a dress that shrank in the wash. When she bent over to help me with the bags I could see her matching pink and white panties. She was able to pull off the look—more like the adorable little girl on the suntan lotion bottle than a scantily clad rock video slut. As we pulled onto the main road to town, I noticed tiny pink bows sewn into the fabric of the dress, making her seem extra virginal.

"I like your bows," I said flirtatiously, shifting my eyes from her to the rearview mirror at the police car tailgating me. I held my breath and made sure I was going the speed limit.

"Got 'em at a breast cancer fundraiser. I made three dresses incorporatin' the bows, all for charity, but I liked this one so much I kept it. I know it's wrong but I looked so ador'ble in it I had to!"

Shawna did look unbelievably cute in her dress. All she was missing to cap off the ensemble was a giant, rainbow-swirl lollipop. I glanced over at her, loving that underneath her sweet, silly outfit was a little girl who fucked like a pornstar.

"You look like a sexy virgin in that outfit," I cooed, breathing easier as the police car pulled off on a side road.

"Keep your mind out the gutter," she snapped, then bit her lip in thought. "Did you know on page six hundred an' sixty-six a' the dictionary you can find Villain, Violence, Virgin Mary an' Virus? If I 'member correctly, an' I do, the page begins wit' Vietnam an' ends wit' Vishnu."

"You're a strange bird, Shawna."

"I'm a strange flower. In a past life hummin' birds lived off my nectar," she replied, pausing a moment. "Can I have a cigarette?"

"I didn't know flowers smoked?" I handed her the pack.

"There's one that does. Its home only ta the rainforests a Brazil. Pollen gets spread through a smoke-like mist. They call it Meeka Peechu, the smoking flower."

"Really?"

"Nah, I made that up." She giggled.

We staked out all the locations I would've visited in town. Elmer's General Store, which had bags of feed piled on the rickety wooden planks out front; Allen's Motel, which advertised *Rooms for just $19.99 a Night, Phones in each room, Truck Parking, and New Cable TV*; Berner's Pharmacy, featuring a lunch counter and antique soda fountain. Devil Kill was such a tiny town that it took only ten minutes to see everything it had to offer. I dropped Shawna off at Larson's Laundromat on the main drag, after kissing her for as long as we'd searched the town. I had a hard time keeping my hands off her. She oozed sexiness from every pore. Everything about her was a giggling aphrodisiac. Her fragrance filled the air like a botanical garden, and I swore that when I caught her in the right light, sun or moon, she glowed like a seraph princess. It would be hard to let her go, I thought. But now was the time to leave town.

I'd collected all the information she could provide and now, besides sex and companionship, I really had no use for her. She'd be missed, more than anything before in my life. But if I truly cared for Shawna, I couldn't involve her in this dilemma. The police may have caught onto my scent by now. My brother and Charlotte were still missing and, from the screams of the message, in grave danger.

So I sat in the Lincoln, a cigarette smoking between my fingers, holding the top of the steering wheel, saying a silent goodbye. Watching Shawna as she lugged her duffel bag of laundry inside, I felt a slight ripple of guilt. A true gentleman would have given her a hand carrying the cumbersome bag. Too late now. I butted out the cigarette in the ashtray and picked up my notebook. Flipping through the pages I stopped on the words I'd written down in Minneapolis from Jim's message. *Children, Tattoos, Devil, One, I–35, Please God No!*

I tried to wrap my brain around the message again like it was a jumble in the morning paper. Staring at the words, I hoped they'd take form between the thin blue lines on the page and clarify my search. When nothing magically appeared I decided to break down each individual word and what it could possibly mean.

Devil—what could *Devil* mean? My first thought was Satanists; Satanists abducted Jim and Charlotte. She was pregnant, maybe they needed a sacrifice? Then I thought of Beatrice, and her history lesson about the origin of Devil Kill's name.

Maybe Jim was trying to tell me the name of the town he was in— Devil Kill.

The next word was *Tattoos*. Maybe the person who abducted them or was after them had tattoos? Or owned a tattoo shop? That wasn't much of a clue nowadays. Tattoos were fashion accessories more common than the wristwatch. There was a time when you'd know where to look and who to look for if you were searching for someone with a tattoo. But now, even the pink-haired barista in that Minneapolis coffee shop had a tattoo on her neck.

Children. My first thought again was Charlotte was pregnant. What did that have to do with Children? Children? Maybe the confrontation took place near an elementary school, or a day care center—or possibly a playground. Maybe the person who abducted them had children.

One. My first thought was of the angry-faced man, Sawyer, with one hand.

I wrote the words down again in order, leaving spaces between them, trying to imagine what could fill the gaps covered by the static and screams of the voicemail.

___DEVIL___TATTOO'S___CHILDREN___ONE___I-35___ PLEASE GOD NO

I wrote in my answers.

I'm in DEVIL KILL a man with TATTOO'S has CHILDREN with ONE hand on I-35... PLEASE GOD NO!

I wrote down a sentence in my notebook. Maybe, a man with one hand, tattoos and children abducted Jim and Charlotte in Devil Kill off I-35?

Frustrated, I started the Lincoln and backed out of the parking space, taking a last look at Shawna through the plate-glass window of the Laundromat. She was adorable, throwing handfuls of clothes into the washing machine. She stood on her tiptoes. Her little pink and white panties peeking from under her pink dress teased me as I reversed the car. My pants began to bulge and I smiled, knowing I'd miss her more than I could imagine as she bounced and twirled, her long auburn hair sprouting out of both sides of her head like a little girl's. I'd pine for her witty banter and that beautiful face of perfect smiles and perfect skin, those glowing green eyes. Shit—I'd even miss her one eyebrow.

I stomped on the breaks, jammed the Lincoln into drive and pulled back into the parking space. Grabbing my notebook and pen, I began to write feverishly.

DEVIL = DEVIL KILL, Shawna lived in Devil Kill
TATTOOS = Shawna had TATTOOS
CHILDREN = Shawna had TATTOOS of CHILDREN on her left arm.
ONE = Shawna had only ONE eyebrow.

It couldn't be. Was my brother trying to describe Shawna? Did she abduct them? Or maybe lure them for someone else? Did she know more than she'd let on?

I lit a cigarette. Dragging impatiently on my smoke, blowing out a cloud of disbelief, I stared through the large window of the Laundromat. Observing Shawna, I accused her with my eyes. A sharp feeling of deception stabbed at my heart. Why would she do it? What would she have to gain? Why was *I* still alive? She could've killed me in my sleep last night if she wanted to. Maybe I should stay in Devil Kill, investigate her house, search for clues and ask pertinent questions to see if she slipped up somehow. I picked up the gun from under the driver's seat, held it in my hands, flipped off the safety, cocked it. If all else failed, I thought, this would help me get answers.

17

SATURDAY, MARCH 7TH
DEVIL KILL, OKLAHOMA

───────────────────────────

What did Shawna have to do with my brother's disappearance? She handed me the bag of clean clothes, my head filled with slithering worms of skepticism she kissed my cheek, thanking me for being chivalrous. I shoved Rocky to the side and piled the bag on the backseat of the Lincoln. On the drive back to her house Shawna was excessively affectionate, holding my hand as I navigated the winding road, curling my tangled hair around her finger flirtatiously while prattling on about dolls, imaginary childhood friends and her weird family.

I questioned her act as if it was just that. Inside her shack I plopped my angry bones on the sofa, probing the living area for anything suspicious, wondering how I could be so dumb. How could I believe something *good* might actually happen to me? My lungs were tainted. More than just a film of black tobacco residue coated them. I was cursed since the day of my parents' accident. I've never had the privilege of breathing clean life into my lungs.

Nothing had changed in the living room. It still consisted of clothes, sewing equipment and dolls. I didn't see anything out of the ordinary. Just girly, frilly things: bows, pink drapes, flowers, a silly white unicorn statue on the coffee table.

"I love unicorns," she said, as I lifted it off the table, inspecting the base of the statue. I didn't really know what I was looking for. On the bottom of the statue it read: made in 1969.

"Why?" I retorted.

"All girls love unicorns. They're pretty an' beautiful an' mystical." She bobbed her head annoyingly as she spoke, "Unicorns are just perfect."

"That's bullshit," I snapped. "Girls love unicorns because they don't exist."

"Why's that matter? It's what a unicorn represents that makes 'em so special. Not that they ain't real."

"Exactly." I placed it back on the table. "They represent perfection, because they're *not* real. If a unicorn took a shit and you had to clean up the mess they wouldn't be so alluring."

"What's got you all fussy?" Shawna turned and flapped up her skirt in the air. Her cute ass was packaged tightly in the pink and white ruffled panties. I ignored her display and continued my investigation. In the kitchen, a stuffed owl rested on the top of a windowsill.

"What's that?" I nodded to the owl.

"Oh, my daddy stuffs animals. He an' I did that one together when I's li'l. Well, sorta. I just watched," she said, staring at it for a moment. Her face seemed sad, then she snapped out of it. "I love li'l animals, stuffin' them seems mean." She turned to me, upset. "But it's about the only thing we ever done together so I kept it."

"You know how to mount animals?"

"I never done it b'fore but it doesn't look so difficult. 'Cept for rippin' out a poor li'l critter's guts. That'd make me barf, ugh." She opened her mouth and stuck out her tongue. "But I suppose, it ain't that different from makin' my dolls."

"One of my hobbies is taxidermy," I said, admiring the craftsmanship of the owl from the sofa.

"I know. I saw that weird thing in your back seat." She frowned slightly. "I didn't say nothin' 'cause I don't want no answer. When I's a child I wanted ta be a veterinarian, but that never happened."

She danced into the kitchen and started washing a few glasses from the pile in the sink, distracting herself from the conversation. I reached into my bag and began going through my things, pulling out the picture of Jim and Charlotte and placed it on the coffee table. I wanted to see Shawna's reaction to the photo. Maybe she'd tip me off, lose her cool for a moment when she saw her victims' faces again. She returned to the living room with two glasses of water, glanced at the picture, and set the glasses down on the table.

"Who's that?" Shawna asked.

"My brother and his wife," I replied, trying to gauge her facial expression. But she just stared blankly, then bit her lip and slanted her head slightly as she turned to me.

"I met them b'fore?"

"What?" I asked, surprised. That was the last thing I expected to come out of her tiny mouth.

"I met them… wit' my Uncle Butch."

"How?" I wondered, shocked she'd come in contact with Jim, or revealed that they'd crossed paths before. I reached into my pack and grabbed a smoke out of habit.

"He liked their band, The Crusties?"

"Carnies," I corrected her.

"Yeah, that's it. He talked ta 'em after a show one time an' they had lots in common."

What could my brother and some hick have in common? "What'd they talk about?" I lit my cigarette.

"Music, mostly. Uncle Butch played the guitar an' banjo an' he had the best record collection. He got stacks a records this high!" she squealed, holding her hand over her head. "Plus he loved cocaine an' they provided it. People don't need much more'n that ta become friendly. Drugs an' music."

"When was this?" I pulled on my smoke, still taken aback by this coincidence.

"Maybe a year or so ago," she said. "One night your brother and his wife stopped by Butch's an' I was over his house. They sold him some coke an' we all hung out an' done rattails all night long."

"Did what?" I shook my head, exhaling.

"That's what my Uncle Butch usta call lines a' cocaine. He thought the long, squiggly white lines on the plate looked like li'l rattails."

"What else happened?" I was confused. "Do you remember?"

"Course, I got a photographic mem'ry." She grabbed a smoke and I lit it. "We just did a buncha coke. Your brother an' his wife, they kept sayin' they don't do it really, just sell it. But they liked ta stay up late an' shoot the shit wit' Butch cause he was into everythin' but 'specially country like Willie an' Merle Haggared an' Hank Williams an' The Guthries, even Ol' Dock Boggs."

"Dock Boggs?"

"Oh, man!" Shawna screeched. "He was an old singer, banjo player, who wrote these brutal songs bout killin' an' revenge. They call 'em murder ballads." A broad smile broke across her face. "Uncle Butch usta sing me ta sleep wit' some a' his songs when I's a kid." She smiled gleefully.

"Is that really appropriate for children?"

"I didn't understand it, besides, all bedtime stories are nasty. *Li'l Red Ridin' Hood, Hansel n' Gretel,* even *Rock-a-bye-baby* ain't suitable for younger listeners."

"I guess." I took a drag on my smoke and steered our conversation back on track. "So, Jim and your uncle." I still tried to grasp the coincidence. "Bonded over music... then he became his coke dealer?"

"Yep, sometimes they'd hang a while an' play songs wit' Butch on his banjo an' listen ta his records. They was real nice folks."

"We need to go see your uncle," I said, stamping out my cigarette in the seashell.

"Well, that might be difficult," she said, overcast by a cloud of smoke.

"Why?" I responded, irritated.

"Uncle Butch… he don't really exist no more."

"He's dead?"

"Not dead, but his brain is. See, the doctors said he kinda abused it."

"How?" I demanded.

"As a kid, Uncle Butch usta see things that wasn't there sometimes. An' when he did, he begun sniffin' glue, 'specially in school ta make it stop. Then he dropped out an' started wit' cans a WD40 from the garage he worked in. He'd pop off the nozzle an' stick the tube right up his nostril an' spray it like whipped cream, my daddy'd say." She smiled as if this was a playful childhood memory, "I thought it was funny as a kid. He got fired a' course, an' began a paintin' business which led ta his toluene addiction. That's chemicals used for thinnin' paint." She dragged on her smoke. "He'd sniff the chemicals right outta the tin can or pour it into a rag an' hold it over his face for hours. Never did paint nuthin'. I guess you could say the only thing Uncle Butch was ever successful at was collectin' records an' shovin' shit up his nose."

"So he went brain dead?"

"Well, my daddy an' granddaddy sat him down an' told him ta stop an' he did. But he started doin' cocaine a few years later. By then, they just said Butch was a sniffer an' he gonna do what he gonna do."

"So he's too fucked up to tell us anything?"

"Basically, yeah," she sighed. "The doctor said his brain deteriorated kinda like Alzheimer's, only he's just forty-five. They believe he had an undiagnosed brain condition when he's li'l an' that all the drugs an' sniffin' exaggerated his condition. Anyway, the lights, they're on, but ain't nobody at home." She reached over and squeezed my hand tightly.

"Where is he?" I glanced at her face. It grew long and sad.

"He's in a home now in Texas on account a' his seein' things that weren't there."

"Like hallucinations?"

"Sorta, the state had him committed after he was convinced somebody was in his house. He called up the cops an' when they got there, Uncle Butch was sittin' in a chair in the corner a' the room holdin' a shotgun. The cops searched everywhere an' didn't find nuthin' but Butch was still convinced someone was inside. So the cops took him through every room in the house ta show him it was empty." She took a final drag and butted her cigarette out in the seashell then continued. "When they got ta the bathroom Uncle Butch started screamin' an' screamin' at the top a' his lungs an' pointin' at the guy who done broke in the house."

"Who was it?" I asked.

"Turned out, Uncle Butch was pointin' at the lookin' glass. His mind was so fucked up he couldn't even 'member what his own reflection was like."

I picked up the water, took a sip, not believing the only person who could possibly help me was a vegetable.

"Now Uncle Butch just stares off in the distance an' don't understand nuthin'. He has ta be fed like a baby. An' they throw a white sheet over his head ta' get him ta' fall asleep."

"Jesus." I shook my head, remembering how I did the same for my parakeets as a kid. "So have you seen my brother recently?"

"No, only that one time. I'd forgotten all about it. Uncle Butch went crazy, or whatever you call it, 'bout 3 or 4 months after I met your brother."

"And they haven't tried to contact you?"

"Why would they? I don't do coke really an' Uncle Butch was long gone. Maybe they stopped by lookin' for him but I don't know." She stood and walked across the room.

"This is really weird." I shook my head.

"I know… ta think I'd heard a' you before we'd ever met. You can't make that shit up. It must be fate." She smiled, grabbing the bag of laundry off the floor and walked into her room.

Sitting back down on the sofa I thought about all the new information I'd gathered. I lit another cigarette, thought about Jim and Charlotte and their bizarre connection to Shawna. She fit the description or clues I had in the phone message. She had met my brother before and knew where to find him. Jim and Charlotte had been dealing drugs for over a year. The cops from Wichita knew about them and were hot on their trail. The more I learned about this mystery, the more tangled it became.

18

Shawna's family lived a few towns over from Devil Kill, just across the Red River that divided Oklahoma and Texas. We crossed state lines in a matter of minutes and cruised along on the dark, narrow road heading south.

She reached over, tenderly rubbed my neck and I realized I had a girlfriend, or a pretty good imitation of one. If she was involved with Jim's disappearance she deserved an award. It was hard to remain suspicious of her, bouncing around in the front seat in one of her doll-dresses. A white doily outlined her plunging neckline. Pale blue sparkly fabric flowed past her waist to the middle of her slender, toned thighs. Two frilly white strips ran straight down from the doily neckline over her breasts making a long U on the front of the dress. Her hair was tied back on both sides with matching light blue ribbons, framing her exotic face as she grinned from ear to ear like the Cheshire cat. Her missing eyebrow added a touch of insanity to her beautiful, sexy, childlike façade.

Shawna became so wound up I had to tell her to "put her seatbelt on" and "calm down" and "relax" several times. She didn't even get mad at me. She just smiled and kept kissing me on the cheek as we drove strange, winding roads that eventually turned into a bumpy dirt path. I wondered if she was excited to be with me or excited about the trap she was setting for me. A surprise waited for her and her family, if that was who we were truly seeing. The gun was hidden in the inside pocket of my coat, with the safety off.

"What's gotten into you?" I asked.

"I'm just happy. My momma's been buggin' me like heck ta meet someone nice."

"Have you ever brought a guy home before?" I inquired.

"Only once. Well, I've had hundreds a boyfriends but only a couple was real."

"What do you mean?"

"I had a bunch a' imaginary boyfriends as a child. I'd make li'l dolls an' dress 'em up in tiny cute suits an' bring 'em ta the supper table wit' me. My parents would ask 'em all kinds a questions. It was real fun. But in the end they'd always disappoint me, so I'd break up wit''em an' they'd cry like hell all night."

"So, have you brought home any real men?" I asked, laughing.

"I dated this boy named Taylor for years. We basically dated all our lives."

"When did you meet?" I asked, navigating the rough trail.

"Well, we met when I's in fifth grade an' he kissed me on the swing set. Then we went steady for a few years. I was the only girl in junior high ta go ta the senior prom."

"Junior high? How old were you?"

"I guess I was about thirteen… he must've been eighteen. I lost my virginity that night." She looked at me. "I know what you're thinking, the prom, it's such a cliché." She shook her head. "But it was real romantic."

"Yeah, that's exactly what I was thinking," I blurted sarcastically.

"What?"

"Nothing, so what happened to him?" I continued.

"I don't know, everybody thought we'd get married one day but Taylor done run off ta pursue his singing career. He wanted ta be on some TV show real bad where they played the latest records an' such. Taylor was a real talented performer, always won the prize money on talent night at the bar."

"Have you dated anyone since?"

"Well, only one guy serious. Took me a while ta date again after Taylor splittin' town. Eventually, I started seein' this older, really mean man who worked at the abattoir."

"Abattoir?" I turned. "What's that?"

"The slaughterhouse," she said, adjusting the rearview mirror, nervously fussing with her hair.

"You?" I asked startled. "The lover of animals dated a guy who works at a slaughterhouse?"

"It's inescapable here. Everyone either hunts or works at the slaughterhouse, or in the butcher shop. This town revolves 'round dead animals. Plus, I was lonely an' he was nice at first but then he started bein' mean ta me an' then hittin' me. I had ta go ta the hospital once wit' cracked ribs."

"What an asshole."

"I know, so Madame Pio, that's my psychic, she's a real gypsy, helped me put a spell on him."

"Madame Pio?"

"Yeah, we put a spell on him."

"What kind of spell?" I wondered.

"It was a harm spell. An' I told him if he ever physically harmed me again somethin' would happen ta him a hundred times worse."

"And he stopped hitting you?" I responded.

"No, he put a cigar out on my hand, see?" She held up the back of her left hand, showing me the scar.

"Are you ok?" I held her hand, rubbing it gently.

"Yeah, it was a long while ago." She kissed my hand and then clasped it between hers. "But this is the weird part. The next day, Sawyer, that's his name, he went ta work an' got his left hand chopped clean off while he was inspectin' equipment on the killin' floor."

"No way!" I said, shocked about her spell working and wondering if she and Sawyer were in this together.

"Yeah, my spell worked too good, actually. I felt bad but not that bad, an' he never hit me again."

"That's fucking weird, honey."

"What's funny is that his hand was never found. It got all chopped up in the machinery. Laurie-Anne usta joke when someone ordered a burger that maybe they was eatin' a Sawyer burger."

We continued driving. The road ended, turning into a narrow path that meandered through haunted-looking woods. This was the kind of area where a liquored-up hick would have a Bigfoot sighting. At the end of the path was a house straight out of *Texas Chainsaw Massacre*. A dead animal hung upside down from a tree. Rusted farm equipment lay dying in the front yard. A corroded stove was scattered about in pieces. The grass was dead in some areas, overgrown with weeds as high as three or four feet in others. An old, dented, rusted blue Ford truck with a gun rack was parked on a hill next to a big white rock. The two-story house was dilapidated. Shutters hung from their hinges, flapping in the breeze. Shingles were missing from patches of the black tar roof. Paint peeled off the wood. Panes of glass were broken and replaced with clear plastic. Smoke billowed from a crusty, black smokestack that ran from a small wooden addition on the side of the house. Some of the planks on the addition were buckling and smoke came out of the gaps in the wood.

I parked the Lincoln and we made our way up a slight incline past the high grass to the front of the house. Inside, the slanted doorway led to rickety floorboards that creaked and cracked as we stepped. We entered the sagging living room. Everything was old and appeared handmade or found: oxidized metal lamps, rustic, wood tables with shims underneath mismatched legs. The sofa was the backseat of an old car covered by a sheet, propped up on four cinder blocks. Several huge deer heads hung on the wall. Their lifeless eyes stared into mine, warning me. The overwhelming smell of cooking meat and smoke wafted into the room. Wood crackled in the roaring fireplace. A stuffed owl like Shawna's rested on the mantel. A wood shelving unit on the wall held a number of other animals: prairie dog, armadillo, squirrel, chipmunk, cat, dog, birds, and a small red fox.

A rumbling, multicolored blur turned the corner. "Sweetie pie, give your old momma a hug!"

Shawna leapt up and hugged her, "You're not old, momma!"

Her mother lifted her off the ground, spinning her around like a rag doll. Thinning, bleached hair touched her broad shoulders and surrounded a large, droopy face.

"Yes I am," she replied, putting her down. "You see these wrinkles?" Her mother pointed to lines on her face.

"You look great, momma." Shawna beamed. "This is my boyfriend, David."

"Oh isn't he a cutie petutie!" Her mom squealed in a heavy Southern accent and wrapped her blubbery arms around me.

"Just call me Adel, or Mystique, whichever's easier for ya," she said.

All I could wonder was what this family had to do with my brother's disappearance. A cold sweat covered me as I glanced around the house, noticing all the deer busts on the living room walls. I half-expected to see my brother's head among them. My hand was in position, ready for the gun, my head on a swivel, checking everything out when a very short man around fifty years old popped out from a squeaky door behind me, blocking the skewered front exit.

He wore an orange hunting vest, blue jeans and steel-toe work boots. Above his beefy face, which was covered in a furry salt-and-pepper beard, was a hat with "MIA-POW" written in large black letters. Below that in finer red print was: "You Are Not Forgotten."

"Hey, darlin'," he called as Shawna ran past me to kiss him on the cheek.

"Daddy, this is David." She spun around and waved her arm to show me off like Vanna White would a letter on "Wheel of Fortune".

"Where is he?" the old man asked, squinting and bobbing his head.

"Right here, Daddy. Put on your glasses."

Her dad grabbed his glasses from where they hung around his neck and put them on.

"Oh, hey there son, my name's Earl, Earl Clovis."

He flipped his mullet, hitched his belt and wrapped his burly arm around my waist, walking me into the living room. "Hey Bo... Bo!" he called. "Bring us in some cold beers!"

Bo entered the room and handed me a beer. He was around 25 or 30 and sported a two-toned, red and black trucker cap with a big red "T" on the front. The frayed brim curved around his wild, bobbling brown eyes. The sleeves of his heavy black and blue flannel shirt were rolled up to the elbows, exposing massive forearms. Bo was built like an ox and had the calloused hands and broad shoulders of a manual laborer.

"I n lu o wi' a mn a tww," He warbled.

I saw a minute strip of pink flesh flop when his mouth opened wide. Bo's tongue was no bigger than a piece of Bazooka gum. Everyone laughed at him like there was some secret code to what he'd garbled. Protruding from his large, wine-colored gums were jagged, spaced-out teeth, each one darker than the next. One up front was mangled and blacker than oil. I'd never seen anything like it. He resembled a demon or monster and had an appearance that would give children nightmares.

I sat down on the couch and, when no one was looking, wiped the top of the beer with my shirt. Then I sucked down half the bottle.

"Slow down there son, those beers ain't free!" Earl Clovis cracked.

"You quit, Earl," Adel said. "What's are's is yours. Earl, check on the meat!"

Earl got up and waddled into the kitchen with his cane.

"Hey momma, show us a magic trick?" Shawna shrieked. Bo nodded along in approval, clapping like an ugly seal. I nodded and put my hands up to say it wasn't necessary, but she cut me off.

"All right sweetie, but call me Mystique when I do my tricks."

"Momma does the best magic tricks, honey," Shawna said, squeezing my hand. "Momma, momma, do the one wit' the five aces."

"Mystique!" she scolded, and pulled out a deck of cards.

"Sorry Momma, I mean Mystique," Shawna corrected.

"Now shush." She turned to me, "See, I used ta strip in Florida, Tallahassee, actually, but my frame got too wide so I started waitressin' at the bar an' doin' Burlesque shows under the name a' Mystique. Then I quit after I had my first born, Buford, from another man, not Earl. My first husband was a real piece a shit. That asshole could fuck up tap water."

"I see," I said, glancing at Shawna's brother's astonishing appearance.

"Anyway, I incorporated magic into my act. I usta wear a tiny, one-piece lingerie wit' a corset." She swung her hands to her waist to show where the corset went. "And do magic tricks... bet you can't guess where I hid my rabbit?"

"What... I mean, no, I have no idea," I said, swigging my beer again. Mystique's gaze shifted down to her crotch, her chubby face coming alive in a mischievous grin.

I nearly sprayed my beer all over the living room as she spread out a deck of cards in her hands. "Here, pick a card." I noticed her long fake red nails had white palm trees on them as I pulled out a card.

"Look at that one an' 'member it good... now put it back in the deck."

I watched as Adel or Mystique shuffled the deck. She handed me the cards and asked me to shuffle. I did and gave them back to her. She went through the deck, stopping several times to ask if this was my card, to which I replied, "No." Then she went through more.

"Damn, none of those are yours?" She handed me the deck. "Go through the deck an pick it out for me?"

I went through the deck.

"It's not here," I said.

"Oh, wait, hold on," she said. "Is this your card?" She reached deep into her cleavage and pulled out the one-eyed Jack.

"That's it!" I said, surprised, as she handed me the card. "How'd you do that?"

"A good performer never tells how her trick's done." She winked at me. "Works better when I'm topless though," she said.

"Oooooh Momma!" Shawna scolded as Adel and Bo began laughing.

"CCCCCOOOOMMMME and git it!" Earl called from the other room.

We gathered around what I believed was a door draped in a white sheet with two sawhorses for legs. Earl placed a large serving plate with a chunk of meat in the middle of the table and bragged, "This here's a fine lookin' buck. Bo got him up north. That boy's one hell of a shot."

"Congratulations, Bo," I said.

"Aggg ya, ju lo n siii 'n de pu 'bm, bm, ha, ha, ha," he replied.

"Venison's my favorite, but it ain't the best meat I ev'r had," Earl professed.

"What's the best, Daddy?" Shawna asked.

"Vietnamese."

"Vietnamese?" I replied, startled.

"Yep, well, actually Laotian."

"I'm not sure I follow you, Earl," I said.

"One night we crossed over the border into Laos an' got ourselves lost in dem hills." He flipped his mullet, then began slicing the meat, "See, we got ourselves real lost an' were trap up in dem hills in Laos. We wasn't suppose ta be in dat territory, so nobody come lookin' fir us. We'd nothin' ta' eat 'cept grubs an' centipedes, an' shit, 'til we fought off some rebels. We was stuck up 'ere an' had these dead bodies all 'round so we cook 'em up good."

"You ate people?" I blurted.

"Wasn't proud of it." Earl stabbed his steak knife at me. "Maybe that's why I got my legs blown off at the knee. Sort a God's way a sayin' we done wrong. Retribution, you see?" he said starkly, then chomped on a large piece of meat.

"Yeah," I responded, compassion in my voice.

"But it don't taste like chicken. People say it does but it don't." He adjusted the handkerchief in the collar of his shirt as he swallowed. "Tastes more like long pig. 'Least Laotian's do."

"Now Earl!" Adel screamed. "That ain't proper dinner conversation wit' a guest!"

"It ain't gonna bother him, Adel." He nodded in my direction.

"That's fascinating," I said.

"See, AAA-del," Earl said, making a funny face.

Bo began yawping. Shawna grimaced, dropped her head and quietly took a bite of her salad, or as Earl referred to it, her bowl a grass.

19

After dinner, we sat around the living room talking about how no one could handle a rifle like Bo, or gut an animal as quick; how as a kid Shawna was only concerned with designing dresses for her dolls and playing with her imaginary friends in the backyard. I caught a decent buzz sipping some of Earl's homemade moonshine.

"That's corn whiskey. Take it slow," he warned, sucking on a plastic tipped cigar and pointing to the deer heads mounted on the living room wall.

"You see that big buck there in a middle?" Earl pointed.

"Yeah, that's impressive," I said, looking at the size of the antlers.

"It's new. Biggest buck I ever bagged, seventeen points," he boasted.

My vision turned bright white, like I'd stared into the sun too long, while I looked at the deer head.

"That's a trophy buck, Shawna. You can count the tips of the antlers, seventeen of 'em. He's a stud, don't find 'em bigger 'an that. Seventeen points right 'ere."

"That's nice, Daddy," she feigned, unhappy such a prestigious animal was killed.

"Did you mount the busts yourself?" I asked, blinking my eyes, afraid I might go blind from Earl's corn whiskey.

"David stuffs animals *too*, Daddy," Shawna frowned.

"Taxidermy's a hobby of mine," I said, pushing my moonshine across the wagon-wheel table, slightly afraid. "Never done anything that size though, mostly birds and squirrels, a couple of my own creations." I looked at Earl. He chuckled.

"Follow me." Earl beckoned as he used his cane to hoist himself up from the chair.

I followed him through the squeaky door in the front of the house, where he had appeared earlier, and down a rickety flight of stairs, brushing cobwebs out of my face. The corn whiskey was making my head spin; I began to think it might have been drugged. I had problems keeping my balance on the stairs, blinking my eyes several times, holding the railing tight. Did Earl spike my drink? Was this how they captured their victims? Was I being led to a torture chamber in the pitch black darkness of the basement?

"You'll appreciate this… feast your eyes." Earl gestured to a shadowy corner in the room. I braced myself, realizing I'd left my coat upstairs with the gun in it. I tried to gain my balance in the murky basement, unable to see my hand in front of my face. I felt things crawling on my skin, bugs or spiders. The floor was sandy, the air damp and muggy. It became hard to breathe. Earl switched on a bright floodlight and I was blinded by the contrast.

When my eyes focused, I saw a giant claw reaching out at me. It was a monstrous black bear, his body hunched, mouth opened wide, exposing large, growling teeth. I jumped back, startled.

"What ya think a that?" Earl crowed, still puffing on his cigar.

"Holy shit, Daddy." I jumped, startled by Shawna's voice behind us.

"That's what I said when he crept up on me," Earl said, hitting me in the arm.

"You shot that?" I asked, shocked, still trying to gather myself.

"Shot 'em six times." He nodded. "Bastard just wouldn't die, second toughest enemy I ev'r faced."

"What was the first, Daddy?" Shawna asked.

"Viet Cong."

I nodded, respectfully.

"How'd you mount him?" I asked, overwhelmed by the size of the subject, still trying to find my vision.

"I skinned 'em, realigned the bones an' muscle. Then I done measured 'em an' made a plaster mold, like they got in them department stores in New York City."

"A mannequin?"

"Yep."

"He's gotta' be eleven, twelve feet tall if you straighten him out!" Shawna exclaimed, amazed. "You should display that sucker. It must be a record."

I swiveled my head around the dark room, still uncertain about why I was down there.

"Don't tell no one, but I made 'em out a two bears." Earl waddled over to the bear and bent over. "It'll ruin the story. See 'ere," He pointed to the bear's back side. "Dat discoloration… sewed up another fur ta fill it out."

"That's cool, I made a few creations myself," I bragged.

"David made a bird-squirrel, Daddy," Shawna said, clutching my hand.

"A what… bird-squirrel?" Earl exclaimed, squinting beneath his graying eyebrows.

"I combined a bird and squirrel into one animal."

"That ain't natural," Earl said, scratching his head. "You're a strange one," he muttered as Shawna squeezed me. I made sure not to turn my back on either of them, trying to decide how to get back upstairs to the gun.

"Daddy, can I have my boyfriend back now?" Shawna asked.

"You sure you want him?" Earl chuckled, shaking his head as we went up the stairs. He mumbled under his breath, "Bird-squirrel?"

Shawna led me outside by the hand. We walked around the hilly grounds. She shared stories of her childhood while we sat on a rock and smoked cigarettes, taking in the scenery. My buzz from the moonshine had subsided. Four broken-down cars rested in the backyard, riddled with dents, rust and bullet holes, the windshields and windows all blown out. Two deer were mounted behind a row of shrubs next to a cord of wood and a large, tan axe with a shiny silver head buried in a thick oak stump. I walked over to the axe and pulled it out of the stump, looking at the blade. The moonlight shimmered off the shiny steel.

"That's one sharp axe," I said, then took a whack at the stump, burying the head in the blonde core of wood.

"That's Charlene. Daddy sharpens her nearly every day," she said as an owl hooted in the distance. Some animals rustled in the woods behind the house and I walked over to Shawna, who sat on the rock.

"You havin' a good time?"

"Yeah," I paused. "Your family's very... colorful," I said, choosing my words carefully.

"They're fuckin' insane," she blurted. "But they're family."

"They seem nice." I tapped my cigarette, sending the ash to the patchy grass.

"Sometimes I wonder how I fit in, like maybe I was adopted or somethin'." She looked at me. "I don't really look like them or have similar... interests."

"Maybe you were," I joked.

"No, I's the spittin' image a' my Grammy when she was young. I miss her so much." She frowned.

I flicked my cigarette across the yard, smacking an old, rusted out lawn mower, and sat next to her on the rock, placing my arm around her neck, resting my hand on her shoulder.

"You were close with her?"

"Yeah, we was real close." She rested her head on my shoulder. "Grammy was my best friend. She died when I was eight. Just before she passed, she gave me her most prized possession, that doll house in my livin' room." Shawna lifted her head and looked at me. "She speaks ta me every now an' then, either in dreams or through my psychic."

"What's she say?" I pried, interested but skeptical of her impending ghost story. "If you don't mind."

"No, it's fine." She smiled. "I like ta talk 'bout her." Shawna kissed me on the cheek. "Last time, she come ta me through Madame Pio, that's my psychic, she thanked me for bringin' Granddaddy ta her."

"What do you mean?"

"Well, when Grammy passed away, my Granddaddy took it real hard. His health faded after a few years an' he was confined ta a wheelchair."

"I'm sorry."

"I know." She lit a smoke and inhaled. "He's a proud man, fishin', huntin'. He was a champion in the smash-up derby too."

"Really?" I laughed.

"Oh yeah, he was the best, his nickname was Merle *The Crippler* Clovis."

"Merle?" I laughed, looking around the backyard at all the broken down cars. I saw the number nine spray painted on the door of a rusted-out, red Mercury Comet.

"What's so funny?" She looked at me, blowing smoke out of her perched lips.

"Earl and Merle," I rhymed. We chuckled a moment then she continued her story.

"He missed my Grammy so much an' sports kept him goin', but when he couldn't fish or hunt or drive or nuthin' he went... a li'l crazy."

"How so?" I asked, shifting my position on the rock so I could look into her eyes.

"He hated TV, bitched 'bout it constantly. He became kinda obsessed wit' it, you know, 'specially 'bout young people wastin' their lives in front a' the 'idiot box' as he called it."

"So what happened?" I rubbed her back. She took a deep drag on her cigarette.

"Granddaddy an' I went ta town an' he had me wheel him into the appliance store. He pulled out his big ol' Colt .45 an' shot up every TV in the store. There was sparks flyin' everywhere. People was screamin', the sheriff showed an' arrested him."

"No way. He just blew away all the TVs?" I lit a cigarette.

"Yep, he had ta pay for all the damages but no one was gonna keep a crippled old man in jail. He made me swear I'd never turn into one a' them kids that sat all day an' just watched hours an' hours a' TV an' eat fast food at every meal."

"Do you watch TV?" I took a deep drag, looked up to the half moon in the sky.

"A course I do." She glanced at me as if I was stupid. "But I don't let it rot my brain or nuthin'. I usta' watch a *lot* when I's younger but I swore ta my Granddaddy I wouldn't. So now I only watch talk shows an' the news an' some movies." She looked to the ground, sad. Her hair fell in front of her face. "Granddaddy was even more distraught after that 'cause we couldn't bring him ta' town no more."

"So what happened?" Shawna still looked to the ground behind her wall of hair.

"He called a family meetin' an' we wheeled him out here into the backyard." She ran her hand through her long hair, tucking it behind her right ear as she looked up. "We all lined up in front a' him, Daddy, Momma, Bo an' me. He was cryin'. I'd never seen him cry before. No one had. He usta cuss an' fight an' smash cars, not the kinda guy who showed his emotions."

"You okay?" I asked as she began to shake. I could hear her voice begin to break. She nodded, as if to say she was fine, and continued.

"Granddaddy said he didn't want ta go on no more. He went on a rant 'bout how the world had changed for the worse. How he'd fought so hard in the second world war an' America turned out like this. 'Cause people don't care 'bout one another no more. Technology made us evil an' people only believed in makin' money an' gettin' stuff fast. Like fast food, an' microwave ovens, TV was the problem wit' the world. We was all brainwashed by the blue filtered light into doin' stuff an' buyin' stuff we didn't even need. As he cried, he kept sayin' he was tired, an' just wanted ta be wit' Grammy. So, from under the blanket that covered his legs, he pulled out one a' his guns."

"What happened?" I asked, nervous about what was next.

"He's a religious man," she said, butting her cigarette out on the rock, "So he believed if he took his own life he wouldn't go ta heaven an' be wit' Grammy. So he asked my daddy ta shoot him."

"Wow," I paused. Shawna brushed tears from her cheeks.

"Daddy started cryin' an' I never, *ever* seen him cry b'fore." Shawna shook her head. "An' he had his legs blown off by a mine an' didn't shed one tear, I's told." She wiped her eyes. "So Granddaddy went down the line an' everybody cried, nobody'd do it. He said he'd give everythin' he owned, even the house he built wit' his own hands ta whoever shot him dead."

"I'm so sorry, baby," I said, squeezing her tight.

"I took the gun, my hand was shakin' somethin' serious, an' I pointed it at his head. I never shot a gun b'fore," she revealed, sniffing, wiping her nose. "I pointed it right at his head an' thought 'bout what my Grammy'd want. I's afraid she might be mad at me but Granddaddy kept sayin', 'Please Pumpkin, I want to be wit' Hazel,' that was Grammy's name. I want ta go ta heaven. So I closed my eyes an' pulled the trigger. Shot him right in the brain."

"Jesus," I said, shocked. I grabbed a smoke and lit it, handed it to Shawna, then did the same for myself.

"I didn't care 'bout the house, an' I felt so guilty I almost didn't take it. Now I like it though. It's almost like I don't live alone. I feel like they're protectin' me. An' it gets me away from this fuckin' insane asylum," she said, nodding to her parent's rundown house.

"You did what he wanted. You did good." I hugged her tightly.

"I know. My Grammy come ta me through Madame Pio, an' she thanked me for bringin' Granddaddy back ta her. An' she said they was real happy, so I don't feel bad 'bout doin' it. But it don't exactly feel good neither."

We said goodnight to her family and they invited me back anytime. Adel, or Mystique, hugged me like a bear; Bo said something, but I had no idea what; and Earl invited me to go hunting sometime, then laughed and mumbled "Bird-Squirrel," under his breath shaking his head.

On the drive back to her house, Shawna curled up in the front seat and fell asleep. I thought about how insane the Clovis' were, but also that with all their eccentricities, they were still a loving family at heart.

"The world's a bizarre place," I said, looking at Rocky in the rearview mirror. His red-streaked eyes glared back into mine. "Maybe I do fit in, somehow."

20

SUNDAY, MARCH 8TH
DEVIL KILL, OKLAHOMA

On the way home from the Clovis' house I decided to take a detour and head to our bar, The Slaughtered Cow. Shawna brushed the hair out of her eyes and sat up in the seat as the car came to a stop.

"Are we home?" she yawned.

"No, I need a drink, honey."

"Where are we?" She wiped the sleep from her face.

"Where we met. I mean, where you said we met."

"Oh baby, I hate this bar," she whined.

"I just need a drink, got a lot on my mind. You can wait here if you wanna sleep," I said, rubbing her shoulder.

"No, I don't want to be apart, ever." She smiled, clasping her hand on mine.

Inside, Shawna grabbed an open table; I slid between two drunks at the bar and ordered a couple of beers. Practically the entire population of Devil Kill was here. The butcher I saw through the window slicing meat, the guy behind the counter at the country store who sold me smokes, the man out front at the hardware store, the grease monkeys from the gas station who charged me $4.42 a gallon, the lady with the bad perm from the bank; even the town cop was blowing off some steam. The jukebox blared an old country song with lots of lap steel and a yodeling chorus as couples danced and twirled. On my way to meet Shawna I noticed Sawyer sitting a few tables away surrounded by his gang from the slaughterhouse. They all appeared wasted, shouting loudly, still sporting their blood-stained jumpsuits. I parked myself next to Shawna, handed her a beer and gazed at her a moment.

"What?" she asked, slanting her head a bit with a curious smile.

"You look so beautiful." I shook my head. "You don't belong in this dump," I said, leaning over and kissing her pretty lips.

"You're sweet." She beamed. "Let's finish these beers quick an' go home, ok?" She reached across the table, touching my hand.

A loud voice screamed out above the music, "Fucking crazy slut!"

Shawna's expression changed to a worried look.

"What's wrong?" I asked, sipping my beer.

"I just don't like this place." She bowed her head, staring at the floor. My eyes scanned the back of the bar; in the corner behind us was the wheelchair-bound obese woman from Stillwater. She was wrapped in a ruffled, turquoise gown with a silver tiara resting in her dark curly hair. She sucked on a Pepsi and in between sips took bites of a candy bar. The wiry man walked up with a beer in each hand and a wry smile in between. He sat at the table, placed the beers down and looked up at me. He stared intensely from under the brim of his white cowboy hat; his smile straightened out as he looked into my eyes like a man who hadn't eaten for a week.

"Don't look now," I instructed. "But behind us is a couple, a skinny guy and the fattest woman you've ever seen."

"So?" Shawna replied, glancing back, even though I had asked her not to.

"Don't," I said, too late.

"Oh," Shawna blurted, covering her mouth with her hand.

"I saw those two at a bar in Stillwater a few days back and that guy kept hawking me the whole time, just like he is now. And I'm pretty sure I saw them at some coffee shop in Minneapolis."

"That's Virgil," she said, brushing her hair from her face to look at me. "He's a *weird* one."

"How so?"

"Well, I heard he just travels up an' down the highway lookin' for trouble. People say he's been in an' outta prison all over the Southwest for God knows what."

"Do you know why?" I shook my head.

"He's just a bad seed." Shawna looked a bit frightened and began to whisper, "Virgil's one fucked up man, an' you best keep away from him."

"I may not have a choice. He and that obese lady seem to be following me."

"I don't know the woman but look at that ugly fuckin' dress she got on... an' those shoes?" Shawna was agitated. "Looks like she done ate herself into that wheelchair."

I peeked backwards; Virgil still glared at me with his dark, narrow eyes.

"Why would he be interested in me?" I asked, flicking my ash on the cracked wood floor.

"I don't know... maybe you run afoul a' Virgil on the road when you was blacked out. 'Cause he's certainly starin' like you killed his prize smell-hound."

I hadn't thought that Virgil and I could've tangled last week when I was blacked out. It's happened before, when I lost consciousness for a period and did strange things, but usually I had some kind of feeling, either a rage or guilt about the uneasy situation. This was just the odd sensation that he didn't care for me too much. And that the twisted thoughts in his head were devising some kind of scheme for me.

I turned my attention back to Shawna, took her hand in mine, and noticed a cute little beauty mark on her long neck when a crushed beer can flew across the room and slammed on our table, splattering Shawna with the spray. I looked to my right. Sawyer's table was cackling and staring in our direction. Then he stood up and yelled, "Crazy whore!"

As he walked towards the bathroom, I stood up from my chair.

"Where you goin'?" Shawna grabbed my arm.

"I'll be back in a sec."

"Don't do nothin', David! He's crazy," she pleaded.

I ignored her and followed Sawyer towards the bathroom. He stopped before a group of people sitting at a table and said something, then knocked over one of their drinks with his good hand and laughed as it spilled on a woman. The men at the table hung their heads in shame. I passed Sawyer and went into the bathroom. The smell from the other day had actually gotten worse. The drain in the urinal was clogged and the deep metal trough was filled twelve inches high with urine and water. I pretended I'd just finished pissing as Sawyer came in. He walked up to me.

"What the fuck are you doin' in here!" he growled, shoving me into the wall. He zipped down his pants. "I got more important thangs ta do. I'll take care a yer crazy ass in a minute." He let out a loud belch and began to whiz in the disgusting water, too drunk to care about the splash-back from the lake of piss. Anger boiled inside me as I walked towards the exit. I stopped at the door, and clicked off the bathroom light.

"What the fuck!" he shouted in the darkness.

I slipped on Shawna's brass knuckles from the back pocket of my jeans and ran up behind Sawyer, punching him in the left side as hard as I could while he urinated. I heard the stream of piss stop hitting the water. It pinged against the metal trough. He bent over and I hit him several times in the face and head with the brass knuckles, then put my left hand on the back of his neck, shoving his head into the trough of piss. Using both hands, I held his head under the grotesque liquid. His arms flailed. He was very strong. He pulled his head out of the water and clubbed me with his stumped hand. I drove my left knee into his stomach, heard him cough, the sound of puke splattering into the trough, and punched him in the face again with a rapid succession of blows with the brass knuckles. Then I shoved his head beneath the briny waste again as he instinctively slapped at me with his handless arm, splashing in the disgusting water. I held him down, focused all my weight on his head and submerged him in the piss until he stopped moving. Pulling him from the trough, water rushing to the floor, I dropped his large, lifeless body to the ground, clicked on the light and washed my hands in the sink.

I made my way back through the crowd and over to Shawna, grabbed my beer and downed it.

"Let's get outta here."

"What happened?" she asked, concerned.

"What'd you mean?" I put my empty beer on the table.

"You seem like you done somethin'.."

"Nah, I just hate this bar."

"Me too," she said, standing, kissing me on the cheek. "Why you all wet?"

I ignored her as we walked out of the bar, glancing back at Virgil and the fat lady. He watched me, never averting his stare as we exited the bar.

Devil Kill was pitch black. The town lacked any street lights. I figured it must have been to save energy, or maybe the town had very little money in the first place. In the car on the way back to Shawna's, I couldn't get Virgil off my mind. I wondered if he had anything to do with Jim.

"Honey?" Shawna said, breaking the silence.

"Yeah."

"What'd you do to Sawyer?" A trace of uncertainty filled her voice.

"Nothing, just gave him a bath." I lit a smoke, took a deep drag.

"You shouldn't a done that." She rested her head on my shoulder.

"Why?" I blew out a cloud of smoke, switching on the high beams as we rounded a dark curve in the road.

"'Cause he's crazy violent, David. He'll come after us now an' he don't stop for nuthin'," she worried.

"I don't think he'll be bothering anybody for awhile, sweetheart."

I turned left down the long path that led to Shawna's shack and navigated the bumps. The dirt road had tire grooves on each side from years of travel. Although my sight was compromised by the darkness, I only had to guide the Lincoln like a train on a rail through the deep crevices, and the slight downhill of the path fed me right to Shawna's shack.

21

Drained after dinner and the bar, I got out of my piss-stained clothes, showered, and threw on fresh jeans and a T-shirt. Shawna wore green silky pajama bottoms and a vintage black Rolling Stones concert shirt with the big red tongue on the front. I held her as we watched the nightly news on her black and white TV. A story about the police officer in Minneapolis came on. He had sustained serious brain injuries and was taken off life support. They had an interview with his sister, his mother too upset to speak to the press. His sister implored anyone who had information about the tragedy to come forward.

"That's horrible," Shawna said sadly. Squeezing me tight, she kissed my forearm. I wiggled from underneath her and got up to shut off the TV before they said anything else about the case.

"I wanted to see that," she said.

"TV's too heavy," I responded. "I'm drained. Let's get to bed."

Shawna followed me to the bedroom with the jug of red wine and two glasses. I propped up a few pillows and sat in bed looking at all the necklaces hanging from the right side of the mirror above her purple dresser. On the far wall, a full-sized antique stand-up oval mirror was next to a small wood table that had an old record player on it. The black bookcase beside the record player had stacks of albums. Some of them were displayed showing the covers. She had the original Rolling Stones Sticky Fingers album. It was designed by Andy Worhol and had a working zipper on the jeans. Next to that was the original Beatles White Album, Let It Be, Rubber Soul, Abby Road, a bunch of Led Zeppelin and Black Sabbath, she even had The Doors first record with The Lizard King design. It was an impressive collection that any music junkie would kill for.

Shawna took out an album, slid the black disk from the sleeve, held it to her nose and sniffed it before placing it on the record player and dropping the needle.

"I love the smell a' records," she said to no one in particular.

The crackling sound of the needle on the grooved vinyl gave way to crowd noise that came through the speakers. A tiny red dot flashed on the silver turntable, blinking like a stoplight as it spun. She left the plastic dust cover up and grabbed the bottle of wine off the table. On the wall above the dust screen was a black and white poster of John Lennon. He stood on the end of a rooftop in sunglasses, arms folded, wearing a white T-shirt that said "New York City" in big black letters. Shawna handed me a clear glass shaped like a cowboy boot, filled to the brim with red wine.

"That's my favorite glass," she said, as she poured wine into her own cup and sat down beside me. I slurped from the edge of my glass so as not to spill any wine on the mattress. Shawna placed the big jug of wine between us and stared at the poster. I swished the liquid around in my mouth, like I knew something about wine, and gulped it down.

"I love that picture," I said, nodding to Lennon on the wall.

"Yeah, that's a great photo."

"Makes me miss New York."

"New York sounds excitin'," Shawna said lazily.

"It's pretty crazy." I looked at her as she continued to stare at the poster.

"I'd love ta go sometime, but I don't think I could live there. All the homeless people, pollution an' lack a nature'd drive me nuts."

"You get used to it. Find little places to get away from the madness, seek solitude." I sipped my wine.

"Sometimes, I think it's almost like the only place on earth I could be happy. All different folks mixin' together an' so much ta do, but other times it seems like a big, uncarin' place full a' noise, concrete an' tar, like we built the one place in America where God can't exist."

I reached into my pocket, grabbed a smoke and lit it.

"New York's about the same as the rest of America. Everybody in this country worships a higher power than God."

"What's more powerful than God?" she asked.

I blew out a cloud of smoke.

"The almighty dollar."

We drank our glasses down and filled them up again, silently deciding to get drunk. I was tired and just wanted to rest, but Shawna seemed edgy after our visit with her parents and the altercation with Sawyer. I began to fixate on Jim and Charlotte again. Were they ok? Were the police onto me yet? At least nothing happened at Shawna's parents' house, so I could begin to believe I was wrong about her involvement. Sawyer seemed to dislike Shawna, probably because she broke it off with him, or maybe because he felt she was responsible for his stump-hand. Either way, I wasn't suspicious that they were some type of Bonnie and Clyde operation anymore. Besides, Sawyer wouldn't be bothering anyone again.

Shawna began to laugh drunkenly.

"What's so funny?"

"When I's younger I loved the Beatles but especially John Lennon's solo stuff, like *Live in New York City*." She nodded towards the record player as the song *New York City* began to play.

"He was a genius," I said, for lack of anything better to say. "That's not so funny though."

She stared at the poster. "Well, I pretended we was married."

"You pretended to be married to John Lennon?" I smirked.

"It was fantasy!" She hit me in the arm, nearly spilling my wine. "We lived in Newtopia. That was a country he made up wit' no boundaries or borders, where people just had ta be good an' nice ta each other. An' everybody was like the president. But there was no presidents."

"Everyone was president, but there wasn't one?" I laughed, confused.

"Everyone's equal an' had a say in everythin'."

"*Sounds* like a fantasy," I blurted.

"It was!" she snarled, a stream of venom spitting from her mouth. "I did whatever the fuck I could ta live in another world 'cause mine was so fuckin' terrible!"

She closed her eyes and shook her head with a scowl on her lips. She was drunk and angry, a side I'd never witnessed before. I tried to console her, finishing my smoke and putting my arm around her shoulder.

"We both had pretty fucked up childhoods."

"Mine was *real* fucked up." She knocked my arm off her. "I just didn't know better 'til it was too late!"

"What do you mean?" I squeezed her again and pulled her next to me, the jug of wine tipping over between us. "Your family's fucking bizarre, but their hearts seem to be in the right place," I soothed.

"I ain't never told nobody this before." Her face grew long as she sucked in her cheeks. "But I feel closer ta you than anybody before in my whole life."

"I feel the same, honey." I squeezed her, bracing for her disclosure.

"Well, I lied ta you b'fore." She looked in my eyes.

"When?"

"In the car, on the way ta my parent's house." She let out a deep breath. "I told you I's a virgin 'til I's twelve. But that was the first time I gave myself ta someone… voluntarily."

Picking up the jug, I unscrewed the cap and filled my boot back to the top. I was gonna need a big drink for this.

"When I was nine…" She turned her head from me, ashamed. "My Daddy, well, he was real worried 'bout Bo, bein' so ugly an' born wit' nearly no tongue. He was masturbatin' like ten times a day an' shook like a naked monkey in the North Pole every time a woman walked by. One day, Daddy come home an' caught Bo tryin' ta fuck one a' the sheep in the barn."

"That really happens?" I was astonished.

Shawna's face deepened. Her eyes sunk in her head like she was fighting the tears, trying to push them through the back of her skull.

"Daddy, he felt Bo needed ta learn how ta…" She closed her eyes and paused as her lips became wire-thin. "You know… be wit' a woman."

She glanced at me like I knew where the story was headed. I sucked in my lips and shook my head.

"What happened?"

"He was afraid Bo couldn't get one on his own. Daddy wanted him ta have… experience, so Bo could keep the Clovis name goin'?" She wiped her eyes with the back of her hand as the tears streamed. "So… when Bo turned eighteen, I's his birthday present."

"Wh… what are you talking about?" I leaned forward trying to look at her eyes, but she shielded her face.

"My daddy forced me ta have sex wit' Bo when I's nine." Tears ran down her face.

"That's fucking sick!" I shook my head with disgust. "What did you do?" I was repulsed by the image of Bo and his jagged black teeth and little wad of pink tongue touching Shawna that way. And the horrible experience it must have been for her. Rage riled inside me.

"That ain't all." She sniffled and continued, "They let him do it for years."

"Why didn't your mom stop them?"

"She... she thought it was a smart idea. They even watched Bo in the beginnin', shouted instructions ta him an' made him do things over an' over ta get 'em right."

"My God!" I was speechless, but felt I needed to say something, anything. "What... what'd you do?"

"Well, at first I didn't know no better. I mean, I felt deep in my gut that it was wrong, but I couldn't do nuthin' 'bout it. Bo began rapin' me every time he got a boner. It happened daily for years. Then I got this place an' moved away but he still come by tryin' ta get wit' me so I got some brass knuckles." Tears rolled down her face and she began talking through sobs. "One day... Bo come in an' he started rippin' my clothes off... an' I let him start rapin' me. While he's doin' it... I's gonna' start poundin' him wit' the brass knuckles an' fuck him up somethin' good. But I just started cryin'. I couldn't hurt him."

"Why not?" I yelled. "You should've fucking killed him!"

"I just cried for days." Her head sloped down.

"Why?" I yelled, rage beginning to overtake me.

"You have ta understand, Bo don't know no better. He's simple an' it wasn't his idea," she reasoned between bouts of tears. "My parents... they done it ta him so he thought it's natural for us ta have sex. I cried 'cause I couldn't defend myself."

Shawna began to sob loudly. I squeezed her tight, felt her hot breath on my neck.

"Fuck." I shook my head, still holding her. "Does he leave you alone now?"

"Yeah." She inhaled, coughed a bit. "Bo's fine... He abandoned me, basically, after he met a girl two towns over." She raised her voice. "Just as dumb an' fuckin' ugly as him!"

The thought of Bo with a woman made me feel sick to my stomach, and my deep rage shifted to sympathy for Shawna.

"Bo an' I don't talk, well, communicate, hardly at all no more. But I don't think the years a rapin' me affected him at all. He just moved on!" She broke my grasp and threw her wine glass across the room, smashing it against the wall, and erupted with tears. Shards of glass smashed on top of the record player. The needle screeched across the vinyl as I put my arms around her and held her trembling body. I watched the flashing red light go off. The automatic arm lifted up and returned to its place.

"Sometimes," I said, breaking the silence. "I think life might be easier if we were simple creatures, like animals." I pressed my lips to her ear and whispered, "I remember cursing God as a kid... looking up through the clouds and sky, swearing if I ever got to heaven I'd kill him." I felt Shawna's warm tears drip on my arm. I rubbed her ear with my nose. "I wondered how he could be so cruel. He gave us just enough intelligence to question everything, to realize our own mortality, but left us powerless to do a thing about it. How could someone give us the ability to feel and understand our pain, to know we're gonna die, but not give us any answers? Then I just stopped believing in him."

We sat in bed for a while as I consoled Shawna. Both fucked up in this strange world. At least we had each other.

"You need to leave this town, honey. Get a fresh start somewhere else, get away from them." I held her chin with my hand and looked at her mascara-streaked face.

"I feel like I'm trapped here," she said, sniffing, wiping her eyes until she left large, black smudges. "I just don't have anyway ta go. I can barely afford ta eat. Family's all I got in the world besides dresses, dolls an' imaginary friends."

"I understand. My best friend's a stuffed squirrel."

She almost smiled for a moment. Then the tears began to rain from her eyes again.

"I got these." Shawna pointed to her tattoos. "Ta help me deal wit' my past."

"What do they mean?" I looked at her left arm.

"Well, this one, the child in the picture frame, is so I can 'member what I's like before all that happened ta me. It represents the innocence a' youth." She rubbed the tattoo on her forearm. "This one, the girl on the pogo-stick wit' the whip, she represents the happiness I usta feel. The whip's ta remind me ta be strong. Like I should've been when this shit happened."

"You can't blame yourself. You were just a child."

We drank most of the jug of wine, sharing the boot glass, until Shawna passed out in my arms. We fell asleep without having sex for the first time since we'd met.

22

MONDAY, MARCH 9TH
DEVIL KILL, OKLAHOMA

S hawna nudged me gently, "What are you doing?" she asked.
"Sleeping." I groaned, my head pounding like a drum.
"On the floor?"
I rolled over, fully clothed in her living room.
"Shit," I said, wiping the cobwebs from my eyes.
"When'd you come out here?"
"I don't know. Sometimes I have bad dreams and sleepwalk. I've ended
up in some strange places."
"You want some water?" she said tenderly.
"Sure."
I picked myself up from the floor and made my way to the bathroom.
As I walked, something felt odd. It was like my skin was too tight for my
body. Maybe my skeleton escaped through my mouth again and tried to
run off into the night.
I did a few stretches to elasticize my skin in front of the bathroom
mirror. Then I turned on the faucet, splashed some water on my face,

soaped up my hands and washed my face with cold water.

In the living room, I sipped on water, popped a Tramadol and listened to the radio. A man with a burly voice came on:

The Dow Jones, which closed yesterday down 200 points, has plummeted again nearly 300 points this morning. The total dead from the tornado in northern Oklahoma rose to 23. Last weeks blizzard in the Midwest claimed four lives in Missouri and Nebraska due to traffic accidents and two other isolated incidents raised the total to six. Police have no leads thus far on the disappearance of the young girl missing since March 1st from a McDonald's parking lot in El Paso, Texas, and rookie police officer Terry Conte from Minneapolis has died after being in a coma since the 2nd of March. Record heat is blistering the southwestern United States with temperatures in Phoenix and Albuquerque reaching 117 degrees.

Shawna entered the room still wearing her pajamas, her hair pulled back in a ponytail, holding a cup of coffee.

"How's your water?" she asked.

"It's water."

"You're talkative this mornin'," she said as she sat down beside me on the sofa.

"I'm hungover, didn't sleep well last night and I have a headache the size of Texas. Your floor's not too comfortable." I rubbed my lower back.

She shrugged, sipped her coffee. "What are you gonna do today?"

"Hit the road… make my way down I-35. I have to get moving. My brother's out there somewhere."

"Do you want me ta come?" She stared into my eyes.

"I don't think it's such a good idea."

"Why not?" A few straggles of hair hung out of her ponytail. She pulled out the black hair tie and redid her ponytail, pulling her long hair smooth down her back.

"Because I'm not sure what to expect, it could be dangerous."

She reached out, rubbing my arm.

"Last night you said I needed ta get outta this place."

"I know, but now's not the time. I'll come back, I swear."

I was worried about this being dangerous. Plus, there was a good possibility the police were on to me and I didn't want Shawna to get involved in that situation.

"I'm going wit' you," she demanded. "I love you. We're in this together."

"Look." I put my glass on the table, placed my hands on hers and looked into her eyes. "This is just something I have to do alone."

"An' I said I'm goin' wit' you!" she shot back angrily.

We sat in silence for a moment. Shawna folded her arms like an angry child, pouting. I began to wonder if Austin was my next, and possibly last, stop.

"Last night." Shawna turned to me. "Before you went sleepwalkin' I woke up ta go ta the bathroom an' your jacket was lyin' on the floor. When I picked it up an' put it on the coat hook I felt somethin'." She nodded to my jacket hanging on the wall.

"So?" I wondered what she'd found.

"I didn't mean ta look but I did." She turned away, anticipating wrath.

"So you went through my shit?" I asked, annoyed.

"I didn't mean ta." She paused. "I found your gun an' a police badge... from Minneapolis. You're no cop, I know *that*."

"It's a long story." I grabbed a cigarette.

"Did you kill that police officer, the one on the news?"

"It was an accident." I lit my smoke.

"Does that have somethin' wit' you not wantin' me along?"

"Yeah, I don't want you to get involved." I stroked her long ponytail. "When I finish this thing, I'll come back for you. Just like I did before... if you still want me?"

"But you said it was an accident," she reasoned.

"Shawna, they'll never *believe* me. Besides, if something happens you'd be an accomplice and I couldn't live with that." I grabbed her hand in mine. "I love you. And I promise I'll come back and take you away from this hell. We'll sell all that cocaine in the trunk and start a new life together. Just like you said we planned last week."

"I love you too," she said sadly.

"I'll come back, I promise."

"This is really bad, David." Shawna bit her lip. "You killed a cop. They'll come after you wit' a vengeance now."

"I know." I squeezed her hand. "That's why you have to stay here."

She asked me to drive her to her parents' house. After revealing her horrible secret to me, she was finally ready to face them. To stop pretending that nothing happened. She would look them in the eyes and confront them about what they did to her as a child.

"You inspire me," she professed, giving me a big hug. "If you can search cross-country for a brother you don't even know no more, take on the cops, an' beat up a monster like Sawyer for me, then I can face my family 'bout what they done ta me."

The sky was bright blue and the temperature was well above seventy degrees. Thinking back to when this trip started in Minnesota, there was at about an eighty degree difference in climate now. We hopped in the Lincoln and made our way south.

A bird gliding through the sky seemed to become petrified in mid-air and fell to earth like a rock. Its body splashed down into the Red River as we passed the bridge into Texas. I watched the concentric circles spread out through the water where the bird crashed.

We pulled up the long path and turned into her parents' driveway. She took a deep breath, flashed a nervous smile, squeezed my hand and exhaled loudly.

"You can do this," I said, watching her chest heave with anticipation.

"I know." She flashed a nervous smile. "I should've done this a long time ago."

We crawled down the bumpy dirt path. The trees rustled in the breeze.

Birds flew wildly through the air, playfully signaling that spring was upon us. The path turned slightly left and I followed, parking behind the big, white rock. The Clovis' yard was just as terrifying in daylight. Rusted tractors were engulfed in high grass. Some dead power wires dangled to the ground from the top of the house. Stripped animal bones swarmed with flies. There were several buckets of deer blood and motor oil lining the rocky walkway to the house like it was the gateway to Hell. Shawna got out and stood by the Lincoln apprehensively. I walked around the car, took her hands in mine and rubbed them gently.

"I'm sorry," I apologized.

"For what?" she asked.

"For leaving you." I squeezed her hands harder.

"Just come back," she said, kissing me on the lips, hugging me tightly. "I love you."

"I love you too. Don't worry, you're doing the right thing," I said, feeling her passionate embrace rush across my chest, filling my body with warmth.

I watched as she walked past a rusted mailbox lying on the ground and up the front steps. Her pretty white dress flowed in the spring breeze, the light blue lace stripes matching the sky above. She turned on the front steps and smiled, like an angel who landed in a junkyard. As she spun, her long hair fluttered past her shoulder blades down to the middle of her back, the red highlights gleaming in the sunshine. She opened the decrepit screen door and entered the house. By the time I got to the driver's side, I already missed her. Opening the door, I took one last look at the Clovis' rundown home, when a terrifying scream came from inside. I grabbed the gun from my jacket and ran up to the house, bursting through the front door. Shawna was on her knees in the living room, screaming uncontrollably. The bottom of her white dress was soaked cherry red. The floor was a pond of blood. Her family's bodies were chopped to pieces and piled in a mound on the living room floor. I grasped her shoulders and tried to pick her up from the blood-drenched floor, but she fought me in a constant wail, piercing my eardrums. Shawna pulled away and fell on her back, swabbing her hair and white dress in blood. I picked her up, dragging her into the kitchen, slipping on the floor. She was shaking in my arms, still shrieking as I held her tight. On the kitchen table, where we'd eaten dinner the night before, were her family's decapitated heads. Between the heads was Charlene, Earl's axe from the back yard covered in blood.

Shawna broke free, turning, and seeing their heads on the kitchen table. She began screaming louder than before.

Dragging her toward the back door in the kitchen, I noticed big letters on the wall that read, "FUCK YOU" in blood. I kicked open the screen door but Shawna wiggled away and grabbed the bloody axe from the table.

"*You did this!*" she screeched, clutching the axe. "*You fucking killed them!*"

"I didn't!" I implored her, as I backed away from her.

"You were here last night! This mornin', you woke up wit' clothes on sleepin' on the floor," she screeched in a rage, squeezing the axe handle. "You snuck out in the middle of the night and murdered them!"

"No, Shawna, I wouldn't do this," I pleaded with her.

"You killed that police officer… You killed my parents… You probably killed your own brother!" she wailed, swinging the axe wildly at me. I ducked and the shiny steel axe head split into the kitchen wall. As she tried to pull the axe from the wall I shoved her with both hands. She slammed her head into a cabinet and fell to the ground unconscious.

I lifted Shawna off the ground and carried her through the bloody house. Kicking open a bedroom door down the hall I placed her unconscious body on an unmade bed. Outside I walked through the high grass back to the Lincoln. My head felt numb and began to pound. A headache ripped through my brain like Shawna's piercing screams had before. In my dizziness everything turned fluorescent, just like it had following my parents' accident. Using my hands to hold my skull together I stumbled toward the back door of the Lincoln, swung it open, grabbed a bottle of pills from the backseat and popped one. Falling to the ground I squeezed my eyes tight and leaned against the back tire of the Lincoln. After a few minutes the headache subsided a bit and I used my hands to steady myself on the car as I stumbled to the front door. I fell into the driver's seat and started the Lincoln.

23

MONDAY, MARCH 9TH
BADLANDS, TEXAS

Dallas was well behind me as I snaked around the slow-moving traffic. The bright yellow sun reflected off the hood of my car. An electronic highway sign flashed 91 degrees, a one hundred degree difference from when I woke in Minneapolis.

Heading south, I centered my thoughts on Shawna's family's murder. Who else could it have been? Sawyer came to mind, but he was dead. Virgil, the wiry man with the fat woman who'd been following me down I-35 flashed next. It felt like he was stalking me, aware of my every move. Virgil was an ex-convict, I believed, and Shawna had warned me he was dangerous. The last suspect was me. Most of my life, people thought I was capable of terrible things. Teachers, principals, law enforcement, psychiatrists—all believed I could commit such atrocities. I'd killed that police officer, though I felt in my heart that it was an accident. I'd beaten that doctor and killed Sawyer, letting my intense anger and rage overcome me.

Maybe after listening to Shawna's horror story about her parents and

Bo, I snapped and slaughtered them like cattle during a blackout. I'd driven halfway across the country during my episode last week, so how could I disqualify this as a possibility? Regrettably, the sanest theory ended with me as the most reasonable option. But how could I have done such a thing? What worried me most was what Shawna said while she was screaming: "You probably even killed your own brother!"

Why did she say that? Was she just hysterical? Did she know something from my blackout she hadn't told me? Did I kill my brother and his pregnant wife during my three-day blackout?

The sun's descent mimicked my gas gauge, as it shrank well below a quarter of a tank. The orange light next to the gauge began blinking. Speeding for several miles I finally came upon a shabby, roadside diner with a 24-hour gas station. The sign on the road was a giant white plate that had two over-easy eggs for eyes and a curved piece of bacon for the smile. I eased the Lincoln up to the gas pumps on the self-serve side in front of the Smiling Egg Diner, about a hundred miles north of Austin.

As I filled my tank with economy regular, $4.63 a gallon, I caught a big whiff of gasoline. The smell reminded me of America. This exact smell was everywhere across the country and everyone had the same reaction, no matter how rich or poor. Each American dug deep into their pockets and could relate to the disgust of paying way too much for something we didn't really need. Again, I was reminded of that sign behind the bar in Kansas City, America, in a word... *Gasoline*. What word could better describe America than that?

A flock of black birds flew in a cloud of convergence over the plate-shaped sign. They broke in one direction, then sharply in another, but somehow stayed together as a group. A waft of perfume pierced through the gasoline as a sweet, young blonde walked by. Her pale spindly legs stretched beneath the skirt of her white waitress uniform. Brown Nike sneakers meant she had a long night on her feet in front of her. A sad smile came across her face as she noticed me staring. Then she brushed away a swatch of hair from her eyes with long red fingernails and approached the front door of the diner. She was just beginning her shift, I assumed, and she didn't look too pleased about it. I tried to imagine what was going through her head. She might feel like her life was a tedious series of events, that she was living the same boring day over and over again, wishing some random occurrence or out-of-the-ordinary action would fill her existence with hope and joy. Maybe some trucker would stop in and take her away from all this nothingness.

I shook my head. If she only knew what the other side of life was like, she'd learn to appreciate her safe routine. The problem with craving the incredible or unusual is that those incidents are almost always bad. Earthquakes, tornados, floods, terror attacks, bridges collapsing, so many episodes that transpired abnormally were tragic and usually accompanied by death. It's like the old saying, *be careful what you wish for... you just might get it.* That trucker she was dreaming about to change her life might actually come along. The problem was, he'd probably rape her, maybe even kill her.

The gas handle clicked and I topped off the tank, rounding the total to an even $80, just over 17 gallons of gas. I sneered, gave the pimple-faced kid at the pump a wad of cash and parked the Lincoln next to a row of pickup trucks. The overwhelming desire to eat got the best of me, so I sauntered over to the diner.

Sitting in a red cushioned booth at an off-white table made from synthetic plastic that would last forever, I gazed out the window. Cars passed by rapidly, a huge tractor-trailer released a cloud of black smog into the air as it thundered out of the parking lot. Maybe Shawna's granddaddy was right about the direction the world was headed. Maybe he'd made the *right* decision. I took out my notebook and began flipping through the pages. An older waitress in a white smock with a large gold cross around her neck appeared out of nowhere. She had a bulbous mole on the bridge of her nose. The mole nearly ruined my appetite. Thoughts of a ravenous tick sucking protein and lipids from the face of its host flashed through my mind. Unfortunately, the pretty blonde hadn't started her shift yet. The waitress I had was a dead ringer for my 2nd grade teacher Mrs. Childress. She had the same style of big glasses that rested on the end of her long nose, magnifying the crow's feet in the corners of her eyes. Her chin was covered in tiny lumps, just like Ms. Childress's. The lumps always reminded me of a pile of Rice Krispies. Every morning before school, my mom fixed me a bowl and I'd stare at the puffy, cream-colored rice grains soaking in milk. I'd imagine I was eating Ms. Childress's chin. Then I got sick and never ate Rice Krispies again.

"What'll ya have, sweetie?" she barked between obsessive gum-chewing. The tick bobbed as she spoke.

I stopped turning pages at the picture of the tree I couldn't remember drawing.

"You okay, honey?"

I was hungry but couldn't eat. I noticed the tag on her uniform had the name Agnes.

Tapping her pencil on a pad, she looked down at my notebook through the large lenses of her glasses.

"That's a nice drawing," she said. "Looks like that spooky tree out by Route 6."

I looked up into her eyes and spoke.

"What tree?"

"There's a scary tree that grows all by its lonesome on a dirt road just off a' Route 6." She pointed her pencil eastward.

"What's so scary about it?" I asked.

"It's just spooky. The ground's contaminated from bomb testing during, World War II and ain't nobody can build on it and nuthin' grows, nuthin' 'cept for that haunted tree." She snapped her gum. "Now, what'll ya have, sweetheart?"

"Haunted?" I replied. "Why's it haunted?"

"When we was kids, long time ago, my older brother told me stories about the Tree of the Dead. He said if we went out to the badlands and got too close, the roots'd reach out the ground an' drag us to our grave. That thing always scared the jeepers outta me."

I grabbed my notebook and walked towards the exit.

"You ain't gonna order nuthin'?" she called.

I hopped in the Lincoln, passing a stretch of strip malls along the road heading east. A strange feeling befell me, like I knew exactly where I was headed. Making my way to Route 6, I turned south.

With a cigarette pressed between my lips, I took a long look at my surroundings. Flat land was off to each side as far as the eye could see. Wild Texas scrub brush, the cockroach of vegetation, dominated the landscape. The shit grew everywhere and was nearly impossible to get rid of.

A lone turkey vulture picked at a carcass on the side of the road as an eighteen-wheeler barreled by. The vulture flapped its wings and shifted his lunch a few feet but didn't seem too worried about the oncoming traffic, either too dumb or too hungry to care.

Between the shrubs was a dirt service road that looked like it hadn't been used in years. I broke right and hopped onto the path, navigating the Lincoln over the rough terrain, dodging scrubland that had grown on the desolate road. Driving into the heart of the badlands, dust picked up beside me, flying off the tires like a man-made twister.

Only a sliver of red light remained on the prairie, making the scene appear dreamlike. I passed a steer skull in the dirt and put the fear of God into a family of armadillos who scurried from my oncoming wake. With the tree in the distance, I eased on the gas as the Lincoln bumped up and down. Jamming on the brakes, swerving into a fishtail, I sent a mushroom cloud of soot into the air.

The tree of the Dead was an ominous sight, standing roughly fifteen feet high but appearing larger because of the flat surroundings. Odd limbs jutted out from the dark trunk and bent in sinister positions. It looked like a cross between a Joshua tree and a scrub pine. The only thing missing was a pack of menacing vultures perched high above. The ends of the branches had threatening bristles, black and brown needles. It was as if a frightened porcupine had crawled to the end of the branch and become petrified. As I stepped out of the car, the dust began to settle and I saw a shovel lying at the base of the tree. I picked it up and briskly searched the area for loose or discolored dirt.

Walking out six paces directly in front of the tree I stomped on the silver steel head and sliced easily into the earth. Loose soil filled the shovel, light, with no rocks or roots to contend with. I scooped up the dirt, shifting it to a pile behind me.

Wiping the sweat from my brow, my week's journey rushed back to me. I'd woke with no idea where I was or what had happened to me for days. And now, I stood in a hole, deep in the badlands of a Texas dirt field, the evening sky growing darker, digging in front of a haunted tree I had, for some reason, drawn in my notebook.

An hour later, exhausted, I stood in a four-by-four hole in the ground. My arms felt like spaghetti, barely able to toss the soil above the edge of the pit. I looked out in the distance and watched as the moon glimmered from the horizon. Placing the tip of the shovel down, I jumped up on the rim, landing both feet on the base of the head cutting the soil. The steel head of the shovel sliced through something other than dirt. It felt like jelly. I pulled back the shovel and watched as black liquid dripped off the steel head. Oil bubbled up from the earth. Bending down, using my lighter to see, I held the flame a few feet above the liquid that soaked into the soil. The light flickered in the night breeze, turning the dark liquid scarlet. Brushing the dirt aside, my eyes focused on the bottom of the grave and the contents buried inside. Below me were the bodies of what I believed were a man and woman. They were badly disfigured; cuts and bruises covered what was left of their bodies. The bugs and worms had done the rest of the damage. They must've been here for a week. Around the neck of one body was a necklace with a guitar pick dangling like jewelry. I had found Jim and Charlotte.

24

MONDAY, MARCH 9TH
CAMPBELL, TEXAS

A bright orange corona gave the waxing moon a vastness, like that of harvest season. The parking lot was alive with sound. Near the garbage cans in front of the bar was a brutish couple shouting obscenities. A steady backbeat came from the rumble of a Harley Davidson engine as a bearded biker backed into the end of the motorcycle line. Two dogs howled from the bed of a pickup truck at something in the bushes. Like a zombie, I fluttered with each step toward the entrance of the bar. My hands still shook from my gruesome discovery. Jim and Charlotte were dead. Their mutilated corpses continued to shock my eyes, like floodlights in darkness. On the drive here my thoughts were suicidal. Did I want to take others with me? Steering into an oncoming car was one way to do it. Did I want to go out with a messy bang? Eating the barrel of my gun was another. Did I want a painless, quiet ending? Swallowing every last pill I owned was my third option. The ridiculous thought of *my* being the last one in my family still living was bizarre. But here I was, baby-stepping through a parking lot, set to fill my body to the limit with alcohol. By the end of the night, maybe I'd decide which way was best to go. If it was the last decision I'd ever make in my life, I wanted it to be right.

A white rectangular sign on the peak of the one-story bar had the name *Outlaw Josey Wales* branded into the wood. *Since 1972* was singed into the corner of the sign. Next to the front door, a blue plastic sheet flapped in the breeze. It read: *Now Serving Food.* In the cracked window was a red neon sign shaped like the state of Texas with a white hot star lit up, the name *Lone Star* above it in blue. This seemed like the perfect place to begin my end.

A bell above the door signaled my entrance. Some old drunks woke from their beers. A few people watching a *Cheers* rerun on the TV behind the bar turned to see who'd arrived. As I dragged myself across the sawdust-covered floor, couples were spread about the place, a table full of rowdy bikers in the corner; one had his hand spread out on the table and stabbed a knife quickly between each finger.

There were tables, chairs, an oil-stained popcorn maker with red baskets stacked next to it and a long wooden bar with a brass footrail stretching across the floor. Behind the bar I could see into the kitchen. A couple of Mexicans in filthy, white smocks were in back cooking bar food and sweating up a storm. On the wall, a series of movie posters featuring Clint Eastwood in spaghetti westerns was surrounded by black-and-white celebrity mug shots and "Wanted" posters: Jim Morrison, Duane Allman, Willie Nelson, Stevie Ray Vaughn, Billy the Kid, Doc Holliday, Jesse James.

A modest seating area to the right, before the stage, was filled with square tables covered in white cloth, black ashtrays, and black napkin holders. To the left, where the bikers sat, was a row of picnic tables covered with long, white sheets of paper. The scent of crispy, fried bar food permeated the air. This was a dive, but it was as good a place as any to grab a drink or a bite, or to face your impending doom. After ordering a beer at the bar, I sat down at a table in the last row, facing the entrance.

Why had I made a drawing of that tree? Was that a memory of my lost days slipping through the haze? I remembered Shawna saying that I was covered in dirt when we first met. Had I been to that tree, digging a grave for my own brother during my blackout? Was I responsible for Jim and his pregnant wife's murder? Why had Shawna screamed that I probably killed my own brother?

A few bills remained in my wallet, enough to do some damage to my liver before I decided how to end it. I went to the bar and ordered a shot of house whiskey, downed it, ordered another shot and beer and returned to my table. A group of cowboys and their dates entered, maybe six or seven people. More people I could do without. The bar began to fill up, honky-tonk music choking the speakers; some of the square tables were pushed to the side, creating a makeshift dance floor in front of the stage. There were drums, microphones, an acoustic guitar on a stand; a black sign that said *Outlaw Josey Wales* in red letters hung behind the stage. Some of the cowboys began to two-step with their women to the sound of Mac Davis' "Lord, How Can I be Humble When I'm Perfect in Every Way".

I looked over to my right, off to the side of the stage. Engulfed in a cloud of smoke was Virgil. A pile of beer cans and a pack of Marlboro Reds rested in front of him on the table. The obese woman was nowhere in sight. Virgil wore a black cowboy hat and a black western shirt with white piping. A red handkerchief was tied tightly around his neck, the bow slightly twisting to his left. His starched dark blue jeans were tucked into polished, tan cowboy boots.

Why was he here? He had to be following me. This was the fourth time he'd popped up on this trip, once in that coffee shop in Minneapolis, then the bar in Stillwater, then again in Devil Kill, and now at the Outlaw Josie Wales just north of Austin. It was more than a coincidence. We met eyes; Virgil doffed his hat, narrowed his dark eyes, a wry, toothless smile drawn on his lips. The wrinkles on his face curled as he blew smoke out of his nostrils like a bull eyeing a matador. It was the first time he'd acknowledged my presence with more than a fierce stare.

I leaned over the table, grabbed the shot, steadied my hand and sucked down the brown liquor in one gulp.

Shaking off the harsh whiskey taste with a cringe, I brought my head down and placed the shot glass on the table. When I looked up, Shawna stood before me.

We didn't say anything, just stared into one another's eyes. Shawna had the blank expression of a ghost as she remained in a state of shock. Her hands were at her sides. She still wore her white dress that was soaked in blood. Raising my eyes, slowly making my way I saw dried blood coated her auburn hair. She wore two dark gold triangle necklaces, the third she'd given me. As I made my way up her slender neck to green eyes that stared into mine I saw a large gash on her left temple.

"What are you doing here?" I asked, breaking the silence.

"I followed you." Her lip trembled nervously as she spoke.

"Why?"

"I don't know," she said as she sat down in the chair across from me, never releasing eye contact. "I guess I still love you." She flicked her matted hair over her shoulder. "I don't want you ta go away… I guess."

She looked away from me, then returned her gaze. "They're bad people, my family, I mean, what they done ta me was wrong." She shook her head. "There was no excuse for them an' I dreamed a wantin' 'em dead."

Shawna paused and her face seemed to change. I noticed a blue vein begin to bubble like a river from her scalp to her naked left eyebrow. "Daddy usta' scream at me when I's a kid. You put too much damn water in that pot!" She pounded the table with her fist, "You boiled out all dem nutrients in da' green beans!" Shawna shrieked imitating her father's voice as her face became long and irritated.

She took a breath, composed herself, ran her shaking hand through her long hair and continued. "But it also felt like it was a past life ta me. An' maybe they should be forgivin'. They didn't deserve ta be butchered like that."

She began fiddling with a white napkin on the table, rolling it into a ball, then straightening it out over and over again as I watched her quietly. I had nothing to say. She began tearing the edges of the white napkin into little pieces with her blood-stained fingers. She seemed to grow agitated again and started tearing at the napkin faster.

"In the pot was a gross green skin floatin' on top like pond scum," she looked up to me from the napkin, her eyes ablaze, "Daddy was so sore cause I wasted those vitamins that he stuck my hand in the boilin' water!" Tears ran down her face as she sneered, unable to control her emotions. "When I wouldn't stop cryin' he backhanded me! Caught me right on the chin an' I heard it crack from the inside a' my skull."

"God, I'm sorry." I reached out and touched her forearm. She pulled away angrily.

"Had ta' have my jaw wired shut fir a month. Know what he said?" She asked, trembling with rage.

I shook my head as she appeared ready to snap. The dried blood on her hair and dress made her appear frightening.

"He said, now you know what it like ta be yer brother."

Shawna looked down and thought for a moment.

"My momma hated me too." She started laughing, maniacally. "One time... when I's younger a fancy woman in town was fussin' all over me. She said I had beautiful hair. Momma got so bent outta shape she rushed me home an' chopped off all my hair with a rusty scissor." She let out a frustrated breath and began rolling the tiny pieces of ripped napkin into little balls on the table.

I remembered when I first saw Shawna at the diner in Devil Kill. She seemed to have two different personalities at work. One was the sweet, loving doll I'd met that day. The other, was hidden deep inside her, but was before me now. It was something extremely angry and dark. We sat for a while and neither of us spoke.

"That guy Virgil's here." I nodded towards his table, breaking the awkward silence. "This has to be more than a coincidence now. He keeps popping up everywhere I go."

Shawna kept her head down, her gaze fixated on the napkin as she rolled the ripped pieces into little balls.

"I have to go talk to him. It's the only way to figure this mess out." She began flicking the little paper balls one by one off the table. "Maybe he's responsible for all this, Shawna? Maybe he killed my brother, your family?" I stood up. "If it isn't him." I shook my head. "It's me."

Shawna ignored me. She was lost in some traumatic childhood memory. I watched as the tiny balls of paper rolled off the edge of the table to the floor.

"I'll be back," I said, and walked toward Virgil's table with a gnawing deep in my gut.

25

MONDAY, MARCH 9TH
CAMPBELL, TEXAS

V irgil looked up from his beer as I approached and kicked the chair across the table from him out a bit.

"Sit down, partner," he said.

"I'll stand, thanks," I replied, putting a cigarette to my lips.

He had a long, red scar that ran the length of his nose. Removing his black hat and placing it on the table, Virgil revealed, dark slicked-back hair that he had tucked behind his ears. He butted out his cigarette and replaced it with a tooth pick between brownish clenched teeth. His long, wiry face contorted as he smiled into deep crevasses that lined the corner of his mouth and crow's feet. Beady brown eyes stared out at me, eyes that had seen and done too much.

"Name's Virgil," he said, holding out his hand.

"No thanks." I shook my head and took another drag.

"Got this in the joint." He tapped the scar on his nose. "A couple inmates here thought I was too nosy, ya see?" He took a swig, "This what happens when you put your nose where it don't belong."

I stared at him, trying to choose my words carefully. Virgil wasn't very big, kind of scrawny, but there was an intimidating air about him.

"At first I hated it." He ran his finger down the scar to the end of his nose. "But now, shit, I think it gives me character!" He slapped the table with his hand.

"I've seen you," I said. "All over the highway the last week or so."

"I travel these parts, yeah."

"You live around here?" I asked, staring into his dark eyes.

"By and by." He took a sip of beer. "Sometimes, when folks ask where I shack up, you know what I say?"

I shook my head.

"I say, I live on the road." He grabbed his beer by the neck and sipped it. "This whole highway's *my* home. You all are just visitin'." He pointed to his chest with his thumb. "I should give a fuckin' tour."

"You got some kind of problem with me, Virgil?"

"Naw," he drawled, removing the tooth pick that dangled from his lip, placed it behind his ear. He grabbed a Marlboro Red from his pack on the table, lit it with his silver Zippo and snapped the lid shut. "Let's cut the bullshit right outta' this pasture, partner." He took a drag and blew out a thick cloud of smoke, "Too fuckin' hot."

"Sure," I snapped. "Why have you been following me?"

"I know you was askin' that bartender in Stillwater, 'bout me." He smiled. "Only three things people want from Virgil. Arrest me, kill me, or fuck me. Now which is it you want?" He winked and clicked his finger like he was pulling the trigger of a gun.

"So you have been?" I finished my beer and put the bottle on the table.

"I wouldn't say followin'. Maybe we just on a collision course." He took another big drag on his Marlboro and butted it out in the ashtray, "See this?" He spun his index finger over his head. "It's a *strange* place. Sometimes people just supposed ta dance, an' sometimes they ain't, know what I'm sayin'?"

"What do you want?"

"The question ain't what I want. It's what you want?" He reached behind his ear and grabbed his tooth pick, placing it in his mouth again.

"I want to know what happened to my brother?"

Virgil tilted his head and thought for a moment,

"Who the fuck's yer brother?"

"I think you know who I'm talking about," I said, never releasing eye contact.

"Follow me." He stood up from his chair and began walking toward the exit, then turned his head, "Maybe I can find what yer after."

In the parking lot Virgil walked up to a large white Oldsmobile convertible with red interior. He opened the door and fell into the seat.

"Let's take a ride," he said, shutting the door.

"I really don't have time for joyrides," I replied.

"Why you lookin' fir yer brother?" He spat, squinting his ferocious eyes as he threw the toothpick to the ground, pulled another Marlboro red out of the pack from his shirt pocket and lit it.

"He's missing. I think you might know where he is."

"Now, how'd li'l ol' me know somethin' like that?" He grinned as he sat in the driver's seat.

"How much do you want?" I asked, taking out my wallet and pulling out the stack of bills I had, even though it was only twelve singles.

"Not about money." He sucked the life out of his cigarette, let out a cloud of pollution. "Why don't we take that ride now?"

He leaned over and opened the passenger side door, throwing his smoke to the asphalt.

"Come on, partner." He fired up the engine. "Way I see it, you got no other choice."

Against my better judgment, I put the wad of bills back in my wallet and walked around to the open door.

26

We pulled up to a one-level motel a few miles down the main road from Josey Wales bar, just passed midnight.

Inside the shabby motel room was the incredibly fat woman. She sat up on the king-sized bed watching a porno movie on TV. She took up almost the entire mattress. The lights were dimmed and the air conditioning cranked to the max. The woman wore a silky maroon negligee that may have been a curtain and was chained to the bed frame by her ankle. Next to her, on the nightstand, was a large bouquet of flowers and an enormous heart-shaped box of chocolates. In the corner of the room was a video camera set up on a tripod.

"This here's a whole lotta love." Virgil gestured to the fat woman. "Say hello Chartreuse."

She grunted, never averting her attention from the TV set.

"So, we got ourselves a desperate man," Virgil thought aloud.

"Desperate man do just about anythin', I hear."

"Look, what do you want Virgil?" I demanded.

"That's the fun part, is it not?" He philosophized, grinning, letting out a shrill hyena laugh.

"Enough of this shit, Virgil!" I yelled.

"Woo-wee, we got ourselves a wild one Chartreuse!" He howled.

I glanced over at Chartreuse. Her eyes remained focused on the TV as she popped chocolates, one at a time, into her mouth. A circle of dark brown goo surrounded her lips like she wore too much lipstick.

"Fuck you, Virgil!" I pulled out the gun from the back of my jeans pistol, whipping him across the face in one motion. A splotch of blood squirted to the filthy berber carpet. Virgil glanced up from his hands and knees, a bloody grin on his etched face.

"You got quite a temper on you, boy." He winked.

"You're gonna' talk, mother fucker!" I yelled pointing the gun at his head.

"Hit me all you want, partner. I won't say not-a-word. Not until you done what's necessare'." He wiped blood from his chin with the back of his hand and licked it with his elongated tongue. "It won't take too loooong."

I looked over at Chartreuse. She still watched TV, popping more chocolates into her mouth.

"Virgil?"

"Yep."

"Can you two keep it down? I can't hear my stories."

"Sorry."

I moved closer and kicked Virgil in the gut. He curled up into a ball and began laughing at me as he looked up.

"I been beaten an' tortured for as long as I can remember. Ain't nuthin' you can do that ain't been done before." He got back on his knees. "Devil's got too much time ta think a' the most fowl things you can do ta a man."

I switched the gun to my left hand and punched Virgil in the face with my right. He fell back to the floor and glanced up at me again with blood running from his nose.

"All this violence." Virgil coughed, "It ain't gonna help you, partner." He grinned, and began singing, "It don't matter what'ch you want, cause time's tickin' a way."

"Virgil?" Chartreuse called.

"Yep?" he said, still on the floor.

"We need more chocolates."

"Right straight, petunia."

Virgil wasn't going to talk. He actually seemed to enjoy the beat-down I was giving him. So I decided to change strategies. Walking over to the other side of the bed I stood in front of Chartreuse to block her view of the TV. She shifted her bulbous head to see around me and continued to watch the TV like I wasn't there. Bending my elbow back, I slammed down my hand, busting the bridge of her nose with the butt of my gun. She let out a wild scream.

"My nose, ooohhh, my beautiful nose!" Blood ran down her face mixing with chocolate, creating a reddish-brown syrupy drool.

"Why in the world would you hit a defenseless woman?" Virgil asked, climbing to his feet.

"Why did you kill my brother!"

"You one sick bastard."

"I'm not even close to done, man!" I pointed the gun at Chartreuse.

She rolled over on her side; the bed began to creak beneath her massive weight. She covered her face with her hands sobbing loudly.

"I'll never tell you nothin' now!" Virgil yelled. "You right where you belong."

"Then she dies." I said gravely, staring at Virgil, the gun cocked and pointed at Chartreuse.

"Hold on, partner," Virgil held both hands in front of him, gesturing for me to settle down. "This ain't the way ta' go about things. You are behavin' like an animal."

"Virgil," I said, calmly.

"Yeah." He nodded.

"I need to find out what happened to my brother. Imagine if someone you cared about was murdered. And you had no idea who did it. How would you feel? How would you behave?" I reasoned, lowering the gun. Virgil stared into my eyes.

"Well, partner, why didn't ya just fuckin' say that from the get-go?" He smiled with red stained teeth. "You come at me brayin' like a mule. All ya had ta do was act cordial."

"What happened to Jim?" I asked politely.

"I wished I could help, I really do. But I don't know who yer brother is."

"Don't fuck with me, Virgil!" I snapped, aiming the gun at his face.

"Look, partner, partner." He held up both hands and looked deep into my eyes. "I don't know who he is. That's the Lord's honest truth." Virgil reached his right hand gingerly into the back pocket of his jeans and pulled out a white business card, extending it towards me.

I grabbed the card from his hand. In black type it read: Texas Style Porno's. Below that in cursive it read: Featuring The Lovely Miss Chartreuse.

"I don't know nuthin' 'bout yer brother, partner. I just thought you wanted ta star in one a' her movies." He pointed to the video camera in the corner. "I mean… we saw you at that fuckin' swinger's club fir Christ sake."

I could tell Virgil was being genuine and realized that this was all some bizarre misunderstanding.

Chartreuse lay on the bed holding her nose. Virgil stood at the foot of the bed in front of me.

"I'm sorry, partner," he said, looking to the carpet in shame. "I wish I could tell you more, I truly do."

From behind me I heard a BOOM and I watched Virgil's head explode across the motel room. My gun fell to the floor as I covered my ringing ears from the blast. Shawna flew past me holding a shotgun towards the bed. She stuffed it in Chartreuse's mouth. As Chartreuse tried to move away, the chain around her leg kept her massive body in place on the bed. Shawna pulled the trigger, blowing Chartreuse's brains against the headrest and wall. Then she took Chartreuse's hands and placed them on the trigger to make it look like a suicide.

Shawna walked over to me, picked up my gun from the floor and handed it to me as I stood in shock. She grabbed my left hand and pulled me towards the door. I saw her lips move, but I couldn't hear what she said as my ears still rung from the blast. She led me out of the motel room and into the parking lot where the Lincoln waited, still running. In the distance, I thought I heard the faint sound of sirens growing louder but I couldn't trust my pounding ears.

Shawna jumped in the driver's side and I ran around the car and opened the passenger side door. On the passenger seat I grabbed Rocky and threw him into the back of the car. He slammed into the backseat behind the driver's side and his head popped off. Inside Rocky's hollowed out body, the stuffing I had used years before was replaced with hundreds of tiny bags of cocaine that littered the floor.

27

TUESDAY, MARCH 10TH
CAMPBELL, TEXAS

Shawna drove the Lincoln south on I-35, the speedometer striking 100 like a dart. The thought of Virgil's skull splattered on every wall of the motel room flashed through my mind. My ears were fluctuating between the sound of air raid calls and muffled tones. I felt the start of a migraine form behind my eyes.

"Why'd you do that?" I yelled.

Shawna just stared ahead with both hands gripping the wheel tightly, a strange look on her face.

"I don't think they killed Jim!" I said, and she ignored me.

It was hard to believe what I'd just witnessed. Shawna was such a sweet little flower. Why did she kill them? Who was she?

Anger was etched on her face. She looked different, as if she was transforming into someone else before my eyes. She wasn't the beautiful girl I'd fallen in love with. Her personality was more aggressive and her physical features seemed almost masculine as she growled at the road ahead.

"Why did you murder them?"She turned her head. Her cheekbones and chin protruded, as if they'd grown or her skin had tightened.

"He was gonna take you away from me!" She yelled.

"Virgil?" I questioned.

"He had designs on takin' you wit him. I'm not gonna lose you too!"

"Pull the car over," I said.

She ignored me. I hollered again, "Pull the fucking car over!" I grabbed her arm and jerked the wheel. We pulled off the road into a dirt field.

Bouncing on the rough terrain, dust flew off the car and Shawna broke free from my grip. As she did, I ripped off the wrist watch that rode up her forearm. Jamming on the breaks in the middle of the field, Shawna threw the car into park, and exited the Lincoln.

Slamming the door behind her, she walked out into the wasteland. In the car, I sat for a moment, sweating and holding her gold watch in my hands. I tried to figure out what was happening. It seemed like the further south I'd traveled, and the hotter it got, the more bizarre everything had become.

Staring at the watch in my hands, I realized how much it resembled the one my father had. I recalled trying his on as a child, pushing the stretchy band up my forearm the same way Shawna did, so it would fit. The metal pieces of the stretch band always pinched my arm hair. I couldn't understand why my father wore it because it seemed so uncomfortable. Then I remembered why. Jim and I had bought it for him on Father's Day. It had a little inscription on the back of the watch face. I turned over the watch and on the back was writing: *To the best Dad, Love Jim & David*. Grabbing the gun from the floor, I stepped out of the Lincoln and walked into the field after Shawna.

"Why did you kill my brother?" I called to her.

Shawna stopped walking and turned to face me. The ringing in my ears had subsided and I stood 15 feet away from her, holding the gun in one hand and my dad's gold watch in the other.

"What did you do to him?" I tossed the watch underhanded to her and she cupped it with both hands.

"What are you talkin' 'bout?" She said, looking at the watch in her hands. She seemed to have calmed down as she stood in the field.

"Why did you kill him?"

"It wasn't me."

"Who was it then?" I asked, frustrated with her game. "I found Jim buried beneath that tree... and his wife's body. You're the only one who could have done it."

"It was Virgil and the fat woman, David."

"Bullshit, he didn't do it. I could see that in his eyes."

She bit her lip and thought for a moment.

"I didn't kill Jim."

"Who was it then? It's all coming together now. Jim's message, the tattoos, and now you have my father's watch."

"I bought it at a pawnshop," she said, glancing to the sky.

"Where?" I held my finger tight on the trigger.

Shawna dropped the watch to the ground.

"I don't know... in town!" She cried.

"What happened to Jim?" I asked calmly, cocking the gun. "And why did you do it? Last time I ask."

"Your brother's not dead," she said dourly.

"What?" I pointed the gun sideways and narrowed my eyes to aim. "I know that was my brother and his wife buried under that tree."

She paused a moment, then stabbed into me with her eyes. "I'm not who you think I am."

"I know. You're a liar... and a murderer."

"I am those things... an' I feel horrible 'bout it. This wasn't how it was supposed ta be."

"What are you talking about?" I thrust the gun towards her.

"They shouldn't a' treated me that way." Tears streamed down her cheeks. "He should have doted on me... like I's his li'l angel!" She fumed at the sky. "He loved my brother... even though Bo was ugly as a mule an' just as dumb." She looked down now and shook her head. "He couldn't cut butter wit' a hot knife but my daddy taught that mute ta hunt an' fish. He even taught him how ta fuck. The way a normal dad teach his son ta drive a car."

"What?" I shook my head, trying to make eye contact with her. My head started pounding harder, I felt dizzy from the migraine, my stomach began to churn and the taste of vomit rose in my throat.

"The scars you saw while you was fuckin' me. Those was from bein' raped. Raped when I's just a child!"

Hunching over, I opened my mouth, a stream of yellow liquid spewed to the dirt.

Thoughts of how she must have felt came to me. A little girl being tortured, sexually abused by the people she should have trusted the most in the world.

I vomited again on top of an ant hill. Tiny ants scrambled in terror. My eyes began to water from throwing up, my brain pounded harder in my skull, like an angry horned lizard trying to crack through an eggshell.

"Momma, that fuckin' cunt, she was always jealous a me! 'Cause I's younger an' prettier than her." Shawna stood ten feet before me, but her thoughts were somewhere thousands of miles away. "She even helped them! Shoutin' instructions ta Bo. Tellin' him what he done wrong an' ta do it again as he was rapin' me. Put yer legs inside a' hers, momma'd yell! Use yer hips more! Thrust Bo, thrust! Pop 'dat cherry! Good boy! Good boy!"

I struggled to one knee, steadied my shaking hand and lifted the gun as I spit.

"I'm sorry Shawna. I can't even imagine what kind of pain that could be."

She began to pace under the moonlight. Her eyes moving wildly as she mumbled to herself the way a crazy person would in the streets of

New York City.

"We can start over, David." She looked down at me. "Start over. We can fix everything, everything can be good again. My family's dead! I chopped them ta fuckin' pieces…"

"You need to get help, Shawna." I gathered myself and stood as she continued to pace. "After all you've been through… we need to find you some help and then things can get better…"

"You're gonna abandon me too!" She wailed, "I can tell! You don't care 'bout me no more!"

A circling breeze blew Shawna's hair in the night. The separate blood crusted locks appeared like hundreds of snakes slithering in each direction. Her face sucked in and she looked so different from when we had first met. Her appearance had become almost monstrous.

"That's not true. I love you, Shawna. You… you just need to get help. Find a way to deal with your past."

"Fuck you!" She screamed.

She grabbed her skull with both hands like it was cracking apart. Shawna began shaking and twisting her head in madness as she cried. She was in the middle of a psychotic breakdown.

Abruptly, she stopped. Her head hung to the ground, I waited a moment, the gun pointed in the direction of her now silent, still body. She lifted her head slightly as she stood inside the spotlight of a moonbeam. The light showed what little white remained on her blood-stained dress.

Lifting her thin arms towards me, Shawna stepped forward.

"Help me, David, please." She begged, creeping towards me, her right arm extended, her left fell down to her side.

I lowered my gun in sympathy. How could she not be completely fucked up? How could someone be normal, if there even is such a thing, after what she'd been through?

Shawna closed to within a few feet from me.

Hair clung to the tears on her cheeks, her wide, green eyes connected with mine. Her outstretched hand reached towards me, her finger tips inched towards my face. A toothless smile arched across her lips. Then, Shawna lifted her left arm rapidly over her head, her mouth, ripped open wide into a scream as she lunged towards me, a large knife in her hand.

"You're just like them!" She screamed.

I drew quickly and fired two rapid shots, hitting her in the chest, sending the knife flying into the desert. Shawna's body fell to the ground, face first. Her long auburn hair spread out to each side exposing her bare back. Two bloody exit wounds pierced through the angel wing tattoos on her shoulder blades.

As I stood above her my migraine intensified, ripping at my skull. I could feel my brain tearing into pieces. My hands began to shake uncontrollably, my finger tips retreated into my palms and the gun fell to the ground.

"No!" I screamed.

The bones of my right hand slid back through my skin, my left hand was now an empty shell. I couldn't stop them from receding into the forearm as my greatest nightmare was coming true. Helplessly my bones shifted inside me like the skin was a shirt sleeve. Gliding across my chest, under the skin, my hands created separation and I felt the intense pain shoot through my body as the muscles tore from the bone. My right hand slid into my left arm-pit, widening the hole so my left arm could slip up and out. Both hands now pushed, running under the skin through my chest, past the sternum, up the flesh of my neck, over the rippling larynx and past the sharp ridge of my chin.

My fingers, one by one, stabbed through the pink gums, and crawled like a spider out of my mouth. Grabbing hold of my lips, tugging back the skin to make a wider hole, I felt the snapping of tendons pulling away from my skull as my head shifted down inside my scalp. The crown of my head began to squeeze through the hole of my mouth.

My skull escaped from the skin. My bony fingers pulled the coat of soft tissue past the shoulders until a warm pile of wrinkled flesh was at my waist. The skin dropped to the bones of my feet like old jeans and I stepped out completely. My skeleton began to walk south deeper into the dirt field, leaving the suffocating restrictions and toxins of my skin in a pile on the ground behind it. The black sky bubbled like a giant glass of Coca Cola, filled to the rim with exploding stars.

PART THREE INFERNO

28

SOMEWHERE NEAR MEXICO

Each southern step seemed to aggravate the brutal heat. The jet stream swooped in from Mexico with record breaking highs. It had to be over 110 degrees. When I began in Minneapolis the temperature was minus nine, a difference of nearly 120 degrees.

As I climbed up a hill of rocks, a scraggly, persistent bush split through a boulder, most of the green bristles had turned brown from the fiery atmosphere. My balance was shaky; grabbing the bush, I used it to assist me as I maneuvered the treacherous terrain. Days of dry desert air left dust in my wheezing lungs. Glimpses of civilization only came in the form of bones in the sand. Some appeared to be human at the bottom of the hill.

Gazing at the pile of bones reminded me that everything I'd known was gone. My mother, father and brother were dead. Even the girl I loved had died, and my fingerprints were all over each death. Why does death seem to follow me like a shadow? It was hard to fathom what had transpired. When I first met Shawna, at least the first time

I remembered meeting her, at the diner, she seemed so beautiful and sweet. I had no idea there was something so evil buried deep inside her. The horrible incidents of her past were written all over her body and they still raged in her blood. It built up over the years and exploded in a wrath that killed her family and possibly my brother. My heart was broken. I still loved her, and I still couldn't believe what had happened.

Peering at the clouds behind me I waited for a helicopter to rip through the sky. Was I the focus of a nationwide manhunt? The police must have stumbled upon the abandoned Lincoln by now, located the drugs, found Shawna's bullet riddled body lying in the desert nearby. They must have linked me to the death of that rookie officer in Minneapolis, and probably suspected me of the other murders.

Surveying the region ahead, I could see nothing but flat land in the distance and a bit of hope. A dark billow of smoke rose from the horizon.

I forged ahead using the smoke signal as my guide. There was no cover to shelter my baking skin, no water for my sandy throat. The grueling expedition forced me to break for a moment. Looking to the sky, I saw that there were still no police copters, just a gaggle of vultures who circled the oppressive sun directly above me. To my right, from behind a pile of rocks a lone coyote watched, licking its fangs, waiting for its meal to weaken. As the beasts gathered I began to walk again slightly uphill until I collapsed to the ground.

I rested my tired body there awhile before I tackled the barren slope ahead. My arms bubbled from the blistering sun as the vultures that hovered overhead lowered their altitude. The coyote was now joined by his pack, boldly standing on rocks no more than 50 feet away. Fatigue built as I struggled to my feet and the snarling dogs became more courageous, inching forward. There was nowhere to run if I could even muster the strength. The pack of coyotes closed to within 20 feet. Tongues wagging in the swelter, their legs crouched in a position of attack. On my left, long dark shadows dropped to the ground as the vultures one by one formed a threatening line.

With the hill of rocks behind me, coyotes and vultures at my sides, the only path was forward toward the smoke cloud. Struggling ahead, reaching into the back pocket of my jeans, I pulled out the handgun, aimed, and fired at what I believed was the alpha dog. A loud yelp went into the air, the pack of dogs dispersed, frightened by the boom of the gun. The lead dog hobbled a few steps before keeling over in the dirt. Standing over the dead dog, I grabbed his body and dragged his remains in the direction of the vultures. Tossing the carcass towards them, they instantly began a feeding frenzy. As the vultures squealed and ripped at the coyotes flesh, I calmly approached. Their attention diverted by their tenacious appetite; I drew my gun again and plugged a few of them as they fed. The vultures scattered and flew into the sky. Picking up one of the dead vultures by its long neck, I dragged it away from the pile. With two hands, I spun around gaining speed and released the bird using my momentum to throw its body close to the rocks where the remaining coyotes gathered. They hopped back, startled, then crept towards the free meal, growling at one another while devouring the hideous creature.

Plodding for miles under the combustible sun, I finally came upon some form of civilization. A 15-foot-high wall separated the United States and Mexico. The wall, under great scrutiny, had been erected temporarily to keep out illegal Mexican immigrants, drug dealers and gun runners. When cities close to the border like Phoenix, El Paso and Albuquerque began having multiple homicides and daily kidnappings, the U.S. erected the hideous wall. From what I'd heard on the news the controversial vote had passed and Boeing had been procured to build a 25-foot-high wall complete with guard towers across the entire U.S. Mexico border. Until then, a series of military surplus steel was welded together, cutting a rusty slash in each direction as far as the eye could see.

Heat reflected off the wall, creating a blur above the land that obscured my vision like a vortex. Emerging through the haze was a monstrous black animal with three massive heads that guarded the structure. Growing closer, my eyes focused, and I saw that the creature was actually three large dogs sitting side by side. Their dark bodies mixed together in the bleary air to create an illusion of one abnormal beast. I'd never seen dogs so big before. Their shoulders were rounded and freakishly muscular. Each appeared to be genetically enhanced, like a bodybuilder rife with steroids. They must have been a special project the government was using to patrol the border.

Either way, the massive dogs seemed to have little interest in me, possibly because I was on the U.S. side of the wall. The dogs had to be trained only to attack people attempting to enter the country.

Their noses went up in the air sniffing at the breeze. Then they sat up quickly and two darted west, one went east at magnificent speeds leaving behind a pile of white bones.

As I approached the wall I noticed the sand directly before it was perfectly flat. Looking each direction along the wall, the sand was as smooth as glass except for the paw-prints of the dogs. This had to be done on purpose? The border patrol probably used this technique as a way to track footprints from migrants who hopped the wall to escape the horrible poverty and violence of Mexico.

Spray painted in red across the wall were the words: *Abandon all hope, ye who enter.*

The corrugated metal of the wall made it surprisingly easy to scale. I reached up and took hold of the horizontal steel ridge in the center of the wall and pulled myself up. Using what little strength remained in my body I scaled it to the top. Carefully, I slipped through wide spirals of razor wire. The Mexican side of the wall was smooth steel, making it impossible to manage. Below me, faded, red dusted tires laid on the ground roughly twelve feet below the base. The tires must have been stacked at one point to help aliens or drug runners leap the fence. I held onto the top of the wall, dangling my feet and dropped to the pile of tires, rolling to the rocky earth.

I was now over the wall and into Mexico, protected from the police and anyone else who was pursuing me in the U.S. But from the stories I'd heard about Mexico, it was ruled by gangs that had overtaken the country. The catastrophic violence and murder rate had toppled the government and terrified businesses, forcing them to flee. As the businesses fled, jobs were lost and the economy crumbled. The latest news stories portrayed Mexico as the most dangerous place on earth, exceeding even The Middle East. Although I was out of reach from the police, the horrible stories I'd heard about Mexico made me feel far from safe.

29

MEXICO

It wasn't long before I came upon a town that consisted of hundreds of small, single-story shacks. Most were connected and ran up each side of the main road. All the businesses were painted in boisterous pinks and yellows to attract customers. The few that remained open seemed shady. They resembled regular cellphone stores, money transfers, or souvenir shops on the outside, but if you looked beyond the few tacky T-shirt stands, striped blankets and minuscule phone displays it was easy to see through the disguise. Their intensions were really for either smuggling drugs or people across the border.

Barbed wire spiraled atop the store signs slashing through the blue sky. The sinuous, threatening wire made the horizon look imprisoned. The signs were written in both English and Spanish, a mass of words and logos that blended together to form some new language. Groups of people began yelling in Spanish, pushing and shoving one another over cheap items at a counter in front of a small shop on the sidewalk. The street was over-crowded with poverty-stricken people, border rats and human vultures that preyed on the weak and naive. Brown running waste filled the sewerless ledge between the curb and the potholed street. The moat was a combination of rain water, rotted food and trash. It didn't deter barefoot locals from trudging through the filth.

Green garbage cans overflowed next to a white, metal food stand where shirtless men wearing straw hats devoured tortillas filled with beans, rice and some type of mystery meat. I dropped my last couple dollars on the counter, tore into a taco and chugged a bottle of water.

Ahead, malnourished animals hobbled through the street. One dog had a tumor the size of football on its side and drank from the moat of garbage.

A series of "wanted" posters was tacked onto a fence between two stores. Photos of nefarious-looking gang members appeared on the pages like a high school yearbook. Some of the pictures had red writing over them indicating "deceased" or "arrested." At the bottom of the poster was a number to call if you had any information about the suspects. Hundreds of black and white photocopied pictures of missing children and people were stapled on the wall as well. Red writing covered lots of the children's faces. None said "found."

A rundown gas station with 1950's pumps was on the left-hand side of the street. An old Mexican man with a white handlebar mustache rested on a milk crate outside, shirt unbuttoned, his brown chest decorated with patches of white hair, a sombrero shielded him from the extreme heat. The temperature grew even hotter when I crossed the wall into Mexico, as if someone held a giant magnifying glass in front of the sun and we were the ants.

"Excuse me," I called. "What town is this?"

The old man stared and didn't respond.

"Where am I?" I shouted.

He removed his hat, wiping sweat from his forehead with a red handkerchief, ignoring me like he didn't understand English. I continued toward the black smoke that emanated from beyond the strip.

Beside the gas station an animal was sniffing at a man sleeping on the ground. It was some strange breed of dog I'd never seen before, with an extra long snout and tail. I could count the ribs on his sides he was so thin, and I realized it may have been some type of cross breed, like a Greyhound or Afghan mixed with a coyote or wolf. When I approached it, it scurried off through a break in a fence. The man lying on the ground had been shot several times in the chest and stomach. Flies swarmed his body and the dog had pulled out some of his intestines.

Ahead of me was a cluster of buildings. A small, naked Mexican boy, maybe seven, held both hands together and begged before two uniformed policemen with black mustaches. One of the cops backhanded the boy in the face. He fell to the ground. Without crying he got back on his feet and began to beg the other officer, who hit him harder. The boy staggered to his feet once again and returned to the first cop who bashed him in the head with the butt of his handgun, knocking the child unconscious.

Down an alley not far from the two cops, four men were tearing the clothes off a buxom young woman. They laughed as they smacked her around, then held her down and began raping her as she cried for help. The cops ignored her cries and walked off in the opposite direction.

"Where the fuck am I?"

"I don't belong here either," a frail man responded. His fair skin was burned lobster-red, and he had crazy wavy red hair. He got very close to my face with his pointed nose and I pushed him away. The man followed me as I walked down the main strip. "Please, I feel like I've been here an eternity!" He cried in a British accent, his face alive with terror.

He wore odd clothing for the environment. His high-collared shirt was white with ruffles and dirt-stained beneath a torn blue velvet petticoat. His dress appeared to be of a nineteenth-century aristocrat.

"My name is Algernon. I beg of you… my cries have fallen on deaf ears." He grabbed at my arm desperately and I pulled it away. "I've lived a poor life indeed. I have abused many things, written and spoken rashly, boasted gleefully upon acts deemed ungodly, explored the works of controversy and renounced God. But I am no murderer... this hell does not suit me!" He began to laugh hysterically and fell to the street. His cackle turned to tears and the poor madman buried his face in his hands as he sat in the road.

More people ran through the streets, loud Spanish music blared, a garbage can was ablaze; a fat, bald man bent over next to it and began vomiting on the street corner. A huge fire erupted upon a hill where the large funnel of smoke came from. Embers were caught in the light breeze. When I looked up, it appeared to begin raining fire down on the despicable town.

Running for cover, I entered a smoky lunchroom. Through the window I watched the embers set fire to a stripped car on the side of the road. The scent of burning tires filled the area.

Inside the lunchroom odd characters occupied stools along the counter. Men with tattoos covering their faces, shaved heads, gang symbols inked on their arms, pimps and whores drank from bottles of tequila.

The room was full of splintered picnic tables, each occupied by some type of criminal or odd character. I moved to the back of the room against the wall, removing the clip from the gun and inspecting it. Nine bullets remained. Taking a deep breath, I reinserted the clip and scanned the room for someone normal to get information from. At a back table on the right, to my astonishment, I saw Virgil. He sat smoking a cigarette, wearing a black cowboy hat and a white wife beater. Beside him, Chartreuse ate voraciously from a large bowl with her hands.

How was this possible? The last time I saw Virgil, his head was blown to pieces. He doffed his hat as I approached.

"Every afternoon it rains fire. Hell of a place, huh?"

"How is this possible?" I stared into his dark, lifeless eyes. "I saw you die. I watched your head explode. This must be one of my nightmares."

He took a deep drag off his cigarette. "You might want ta take a seat for this one, partner."

"I saw your head blown all over that motel room!"

Virgil motioned for me to sit down across from him and I did. He handed me a cigarette and offered a light. I placed the smoke between my lips and leaned into the flame.

"Shit, I'm gonna catch a serious whoopin' for tellin' you this... guess it don't matter much now, though. You see her?" He nodded to Chartreuse. "She's a sinner." I looked over at Chartreuse as she piled food into her mouth with both hands, the same mouth I saw eat a shotgun blast. "Can't stop herself. That's gluttony. Ate herself into that wheelchair, ate herself ta fuckin' death. Not only that, but she sold her big-ass in porn ta make money for food. She ain't never learned."

"She's dead?"

"Pushin' up daisies... just like you." Virgil winked.

"I'm dead?" I touched my chest with my hands. "I don't feel dead... What the fuck are you talking about?"

"Relax," Virgil said. "You bought the farm two weeks ago. An' those three days you been missin' since you woke up in Minnesota... that was the transition."

"This doesn't make sense." I shook my head.

"How else can you explain me shootin' the shit wit' you right now?" Virgil held his hand like a gun and simulated being shot in the head.

"Who are you?"

He blew out a cloud of smoke.

"'Member when I said ta you in that bar that I should give a tour?"

I nodded my head as he continued.

"Well, that's precisely what I do. I provide tours a' the afterlife for those who can't find their way. If you commit the same atrocities you done durin' life I leave you in the realm that's proper." He flicked the sparkling remains of his cigarette across the room hitting a rat at the base of a garbage can.

"This one." He nodded again in Chartreuse's direction as she sucked up a long worm. "She's had her chances ta convert an' failed every test. So this is her last stop... for all eternity."

"Where am I?"

"Where ya think?" Virgil raised his eyebrows.

I glanced around the room at the despair, saw fire in the street.

"Hell." I said, still in disbelief.

"This here's almost the pit. But you've been in Hell nearly two weeks. Wrath started when you passed the Red River into Texas."

"This is bullshit! What happened to my brother? What happened to Jim?" I yelled.

"Your brother's not dead... as far as I know. This is all part a' the ride. Everyone's got demons or ghosts, an' everyone's got their own personal journey. This one's yours." Virgil smiled, then winked and made a clicking noise with his mouth.

"This doesn't make sense! What about Shawna? That was real... I know it was."

"Shawna... she's a fallen angel, and a nasty one at that. Murdered her whole family wit' an axe two days before Christmas nineteen seventy-five, then killed herself. Now she's banished."

Images of Shawna flooded my mind. Everything she owned was old. Her records were all classics, her concert t-shirts authentic, her turquoise vintage Singer sewing machine, the television set was ancient and black and white, even her unicorn statue was from 1969.

"So she was crazy?" I struggled out the words, staring at a pile of cockroaches crawling over one another on the sandy floor.

"Sort a'. See, as soon as she crossed over the Red River ta leave her territory an' enter wrath, well, that's when she went hog wild. In Hell, the further south ya travel, the more ya succumb ta your sinful desires an' emotions. An' the more you do, the more intense an' horrible your nightmare becomes. Its sort a' why they call it torture, partner."

"So she's not real then?" I looked up at my smoke and watched the long ash as it burned to the filter.

"Oh, Shawna's real. In 1957 she was marked at birth ta be an angel when she passed on. Born the sweetest most beautiful flower the world could ever know. But her family was jealous an' tormented her. So much, she committed the two atrocities an angel can't do. Murder an' suicide." Virgil took a sip off his beer and continued. "Because she was marked ta be an angel they didn't sentence her ta Hell for her sins. She got a job like me."

"What do you mean a job?"

"Shawna was one a' yer tests… lust. An' you failed that one worse than a faggot in a pie-eatin' contest."

My hand shook as I dropped the cigarette filter to the ground. The roaches swarmed thinking it was food.

"If I'm dead… and this bullshit's real and not some nightmare… did you lead me here?" I asked.

"I kept an eye on yer soul. See, partner, you're just about dancin' on the end of a rope."

"Why am I here? Why am I in hell?" I pleaded.

"I'm so tired a' that fuckin' question. Let me ask you one." He pointed his finger at me. "Since you've been in the joint," he circled his index finger above his head, "what've you done?"

"I don't know… I didn't even know where I was. This whole thing is so…" I glanced around the room and saw an emaciated man fingering a festering wound on his neck. "Foreign to me."

"I'll tell you what ya done," he said, a bit irritated. He began counting off on his fingers. "You got zero control over that temper a' yours, you stole, abused drugs, alcohol, given in ta every carnal desire you done had in yer head an' pecker, not ta mention beaten people, killed people, an' ya even admitted that you don't believe in God!" Virgil lifted his hat and wiped his brow with his hand. "Christ, I hate this place… too damn hot."

"I didn't kill anyone for no reason. That cop was an accident, Sawyer was evil. That doctor deserved a beating, he was molesting children. And Shawna, she attacked me!" I rattled off my defense.

"It ain't up for discussion, partner. It's zero hour. Time ta be a man an' take account a' yer actions."

"Who the fuck are you!" I questioned, leaping across the table grabbing Virgil by his shirt, ripping him out of his seat.

"Mind that temper, boy," he said.

"Who the hell are you to judge me?" I yelled.

Virgil grabbed my wrists, breaking my grasp and pushed me away, pointing his skinny, crooked finger in my face.

"I ain't no saint neither!" He yelled, "I'm here for a fuckin' reason. Doin' a shitty job I been assigned. You think I like hangin' out with souls like this?" He gestured to Chartreuse. "Think I enjoy Limbo… freezin' my ass off in Minnesota? Shit, boy, Des Moines got ta be the most borin' fuckin' place ta ever exist. An' then, as a fuckin' bonus, I get ta come ta Mexico!" He grabbed his beer off the table and took a swig. "Shit, partner, we all got fuckin' problems."

There was no response in my head that made sense because nothing made sense. If I believed anything Virgil said was true, the situations I was in called for extreme actions. Although each had different scenarios I could have chosen other than hurting people. I sat back down and hung my head, overwhelmed by what was happening.

After a moment Virgil knocked on the table with his ring. I looked up.

"You done whinin'? I know this is a lot ta drop on a young man." He pulled out two cigarettes and placed them between his lips, lit them with the Zippo and gave one to me. "I like you, partner. Ya got guts. Ya don't take shit an' yer loyal. Those qualities are scarce 'round these parts. Shit, they're scarce anywhere."

He pulled a gold triangular ring off and handed it to me.

"What's this?" I took the ring in my hand.

"Things on your journey ever give you a feelin' a' déjà vu?"

"Yeah." I nodded. "Certain people and places... it felt like I'd seen them or been there before."

"I thought you might. That's 'bout as common as a talkin' goat. Most folks just go through Hell wit' tunnel vision." He pointed straight ahead. "They got no chance ta reform. Pay attention ta that feelin' an' maybe this ring will help remind you ta keep yer sins in check from here on out. Just like that necklace Shawna gave you."

I looked down and grabbed the necklace she'd blessed with a kiss after we met.

"Contrary ta popular belief, some a' us don't want ya ta end up here, partner. Even if their job *is* ta tempt ya."

"Thanks," I said, looking into Virgil's eyes.

30

HELL

I made my way down a narrowing street as people, like rats, watched from each side. A whorehouse was on the right at the edge of town. The girls leaned over the railing, calling out to me. For a moment I forgot I was in Hell. They began pulling up their skirts. One showed me her breasts. The breeze blew their soft scent my way and I felt myself uncontrollably moving toward the front steps. I glanced down at my hand, focused on Virgil's ring, and took two steps back. Although each woman was incredibly desirable, I fought the urge and walked away. I looked back as they called to me and noticed they each had some type of deformity. One was missing her eyes, another was bald with a scar across her head, one was missing her mouth, another had no legs. By fighting off the temptation I was able to see their true nature. They were demons, or traps, to lure me further into despondency.

The charred land began to rise as I passed a row of scorched trees. Swarms of bugs and moths polluted the syrupy air as the rabid heat continued. I realized my body would never adjust. This was constant agony, like my nerves had burned off and been replaced with fresh ones, only to have them singed again.

The rank air stung my eyes and sinuses with a sulfuric flare. As the hill became steeper and steeper the fires burned hotter, I looked back at the tiny lights of the town; I was now on a mountain. The dark ground grew rockier, the elevation pulled at my lungs as I ascended towards the peak.

Time meant nothing here because everything took forever. When I reached the apex there was no other side of the mountain, only blackness. A massive hole sat at the top like a dormant volcano. As I crept over the edge into the dark I found spiral steps of flint hugging the inner wall of the volcano, and I made the descent into the giant void. Stumbling, nearly falling into the abyss several times, I found a stick on the ground. Tearing part of my T-shirt and wrapping it around the stick, I lit the rag on fire with my lighter. All along the path were bones of man and creature. I traveled downward for what seemed like hours. The air grew thicker and colder the further I delved into the volcano. When I finally came upon the bottom I found a large lake.

Shivering, with nowhere else to turn, I stepped onto the water and found solid footing. The lake was frozen solid. Walking onto the ice, and peering down, I saw a hand. As I got closer the fingers moved and I jumped back. Bending over, I leaned in with the flame and saw people frozen in the lake of ice. Their eyes were open, shifting in horror as their bodies remained petrified. I had reached the pit of Hell.

Before I could run, the ice beneath my feet melted, and, like quicksand, the more I struggled, the faster it sucked me in. Drifting lower and lower into the lake, screaming, clawing at the slush, I sank deeper and deeper, past the bodies of others. The slush around me began to solidify and I was suspended, mouth open wide in mid scream. The ice encased my body leaving no room to move. I felt the cold begin to burn my skin even worse than the scorching heat I experienced before. Unable to move, trapped in place, I was left with the least amount of air possible to breath in my frozen cocoon. Only enough to bareley function.

Continuous pain and suffering befell me. The constant feeling as if each breath would be my last, my throat dry as the desert, yet I was surrounded by solid water that never dripped. Claustrophobia set in and I felt torture in its fullest and simplest form. My mind went mad. I was frozen alive for eternity in the terrifying and suffocating moment a man experiences before he died.

Like the others I had seen through the ice, my eyes were frozen wide open. It was a nightmare worse than any insomniac could fathom. Even air was against me. Never making it fully into my lungs, it teased me with short breath as I silently tried to moan and fight. The more I contested the more intense the physical and psychological pain became. The only hope was for death.

It felt like years, maybe decades that I remained in this state, tortured in ice so cold my fingers could snap like twigs in the slightest breeze. I was left with only my insane thoughts and a desperate prayer, that the claustrophobic ice that imprisoned me, would somehow retreat just enough so I could smash my skull into it until I died.

Then, a divine dream came to me. The ice began to transform, thawing the frozen lake as it had long before when I was snared in this trap. I felt my body begin to slip downward. As I did, my eyes finally loosened, and I closed them to sleep.

31

The first glimmer of sunlight peeked above the landscape. I awoke, on the backseat of my grandfather's old Lincoln Continental surrounded by small white pills, food wrappers and empty beer cans. Shaking and bleary-eyed, I felt the cold air encircle me. My right calf ached as I stretched it along the plush maroon leather of the backseat.

"Where am I?" I said aloud.

"You're in Minnesota, partner."

An older man with a black cowboy hat, tanned skin, and a toothpick between his brown teeth responded from the front passenger's seat.

"Who the fuck are you?" I asked, shaking the cobwebs from my head.

"You don't 'member pickin' me up?" He grinned, the wrinkles in his face scrunch up.

"I don't know... I mean, I don't think so." I rubbed the crust from my eyes, trying to decipher if this was real or if I was trapped in a dream.

"Names Virgil," The man held his hand out and I shook it. "You picked me up last night hitchhikin' an' said somethin' 'bout yer brother bein' missin.'"

"Jim?" I wondered, "I haven't seen him in years."

Virgil cracked open a beer and offered it to me. I reached out and he handed it to me through the seats.

"Looks like you on a bender or road trip an' got yer self embroiled in a mystery." Virgil turned the ignition, from the passenger's side and cranked the heat to max. "I hate Minnesota… too damn cold."

Outside a fortress of snow embankments encased the small gravel parking lot behind a rundown apartment complex. I tried to sip the beer but most of the liquid was frozen solid. Shuddering from the cold like it was a terrifying memory, I rubbed my stiff neck, attributing the soreness to the confined sleeping quarters or, perhaps, the hunched driving position I had assumed all night. For the life of me, I could not remember how I'd gotten here.

Virgil removed the toothpick and tossed it to the fuzzy maroon floor. He grabbed two smokes from his pack and placed them between his lips. With his Zippo he lit them both and handed one back to me.

"Breakfast a' champions ya got there, partner."

I grabbed the cigarette in my other hand and took a drag. The dizzy specter of a migraine lingered between my ears. I must have had one last night, which would explain why my pills were strewn all over the backseat. Sometimes when I get a migraine real bad I drink some beers to help the painkillers kick in faster. From the amount of empty cans and pills on the seat it looked like I'd had enough of both to kill a horse. I shut my eyes for a moment, lightheaded from the nicotine. In the darkness behind my eyelids, little lights flickered like stars.

The End